The Wrong Choice
(Le Choix erroné)

by Luke Jackson

49,400 words

"Justice pour nous, justice pour tous; raison et liberté pour nous, raison et liberté pour tous."

C'est une bonne idée (March 1861)

"Jean! Jean-Paul!" Jacque's urgent cry came from behind me for what seemed like the hundredth time. As I had done some 99 times already, I continued to press my way forward through the deep snow, not looking back.

At first Jacque's whining voice had been simply another minor annoyance, like the snow itself that fell a dead weight on my arms and shoulders and crept over the tops of my boots to melt within. Our horse-drawn tram had been obliged by the unexpected and unwanted snowfall to stop halfway up University Hill forcing the rest of the passengers and I to step down and make the rest of the way to our various destinations on foot.

For a block or so, I'd enjoyed the exercise, but gradually as the falling snow forced its way into my boots, welding my socks to my feet in a sodden mass, I could only grimace and make the best of it. Glancing at my pocket watch didn't help. Indeed, it served only to make me more irritable and more determined to press on.

Soon enough, I reached the campus where, thankfully, a half dozen or so pairs of boots preceding mine had partially cleared a path through the snow. Alas, the cleared path provided Jacque with a similar advantage and soon he was at my shoulder.

"Jean-Paul!"

I ignored him; I had no alternative; Professor Hamilton always had the proctors lock the doors a minute past the hour to discourage late arrivals. I had several minutes still to spare, but I knew from past experience that a moment's conversation with Jacque would soon become five, then ten, and finally an entire hour would be lost in fruitless discussion.

(And, to be honest, I did not want to be seen with him. My own clothes were barely acceptable by college standards, while Jacque's were those of a clochard, a colorful tramp perhaps, but still a tramp. It was bad enough that I must arrive at McGill's gates by tram, while others came by private carriage.)

Jacque was not Paul's LaPluffe's Christian name, much less that given him at his Confirmation, but rather what we had come to call him over the years, because the cry « j'accuse » so often came from his lips. No cause was too small, no slight at English hands too trivial to be ignored. This had led to his first joining the Institut Canadien de Montréal (dragging me unwillingly behind him) then being ejected from it a month later as being too disruptive (and we were a society much given to debate). I remained a member as much because the Institute offered excellent library facilities as because of my belief in its cause: Justice pour nous, justice pour tous; raison et liberté pour nous, raison et liberté pour tous.

Sure enough, once Jacque stood breathless on the path before me, clad as always in flamboyant, but ill-fitting clothes, he waved a handbill in my face. Silently, I took it from him and began to read, more to avoid his harangue than due to any interest in its contents.

Senator Clay of The Confederate States of America was to lecture the following evening on "The Mutual Interests of Two Great Countries." What interested me most about this announcement (apart from the quality of the paper it was printed on, a step or so above the thin greasy sheets that Jacque and his comrades normally made use of) was the location of the lecture. The village of Westmont in Cote

St. Andre was home to the most well to do and the most detestable of our English conquers. I could no more imagine Jacque going to Westmont, than I could picture him standing at attention for "God Save the Queen."

Indeed, it was a major accomplishment for him to have ventured as far west in our city as the university where, to his amazement, I have studied English literature for the past two years. Jacque's own legal studies, begun with such enthusiasm two years before, had gradually been abandoned as the separatist fever overcame him. (Or perhaps the constant need to commute to and from Ville de Québec to attend Laval, the sole French-speaking university in Bas Canada, had erased his desire for an education.)

For Jacque, our province's defeat on the Plains of Abraham a century before was a criminal act that still cried out for remedy and revenge.

The fact I had chosen to study the literature of the conqueror, of Shakespeare, Milton, and Dryden was a truth he had yet to come to grips with. Never mind that he had only studied the works of Corneille and Racine in our years at the *école secondaire* because the curriculum had been forced upon him. For Jacque, France and England were equally detestable. Had France not abandoned us in our hour of need? Let their own provincial concerns take precedence over the needs of their American colonies? Never mind that France had had a revolution and two emperors in the intervening years; in Jacque's eyes, their guilt remained.

"You plan to go to this lecture?" I asked. "You want me to accompany you?"

I heard a bell, heard an imaginary door close; I had lingered too long on the path and my class on 16th Century British History and England's long Civil War had begun without me. To the south, another civil war was in progress, the war of whose purpose Senator Clay was to speak. Though I was not as passionate in my beliefs as Jacque, still the immediacy of the War Between the States, of any war where a young man might prove himself a hero, appealed to me.

3

"No, no." Jacque moved closer; he gripped my arm as though I might run away, though I was now almost as wrapped up in the dream as he.

"We will go instead to the hotel where this Senator Clay is staying. We will appeal to him directly."

Of course, Jacque's "we," meant Jacque alone would voice this appeal. My role, as always when English-speakers were involved, would be that of interpreter, Moses translating the words of God to man. Did I really want to be part of Jacque's latest madness?

"Why should this Senator help? What can we the working people of Quebec offer him? He speaks in Westmont because it is there the rich English live, men of means who can finance the campaigns of his Confederacy. We can not give him money."

"We will not give him money, we will give him men: A brigade, a battalion, a division ready to fight for his cause."

"And why should our people be willing do that?"

"So that the Confederates in their turn will fight for our independence."

I will be honest. This was the very first time a suggestion of Jacques or his like-minded companions had made the slightest sense to me. Immédiatement, I, too had the vision. The Yankees and I would fight side by side and drive the English from our land.

From Jacque's smile, I could see that he shared my thoughts. Did he also share my fears? It would be many battles and many deaths before we achieved our dream.

The next morning, bright and far too early, we took the trolley to the Hotel Rasco despite the slight prospect of our actually getting to meet with Senator Clay.

Had it been up to Jacque, we would have gone the previous day. But I had pointed out the obvious. His touque—better suited to a child than a man, his ragged clothes—his sweater had holes in it, did not inspire trust. And his untrimmed hair and unkempt beard were unlikely to gain him entrance to the hotel, much less to the Senator's private chambers.

Appropriately dressed with Jacque combed and groomed in a manner that my mother would have approved, we did get inside the hotel. And though the front desk denied all knowledge of Senator Clay, a hotel maid was easily persuaded by Jacque to provide the information. But, of course, we were met at the door of the hotel room by an officious secretary.

Told we needed an appointment, Jacque tried to bull his way into the room. I was barely holding him back, when a cultured voice from within said to let us inside.

Two men sat a small table, where one of the pair, the older, white-haired gentleman whose voice we'd heard, was enjoying breakfast. Still more plates with bacon, ham, and stacks of hotcakes lay untouched on the trolley, and I could see Jacque eying them hungrily. I hoped he would restrain himself. We never seemed to get enough food in those days, would be willing to eat meal after meal could we only afford it. Who would have dreamed that things were only going to get worse for us, not better?

The white-haired gentleman, a large white napkin tucked beneath his wing collar, heard Jacque (as translated by me) out, but then shook his head sadly. "We would appreciate any help you gentleman might offer, but I simply cannot promise you future aid on our part. Indeed, just the opposite.

"Our General Beauregard would eagerly welcome you all under his command. I can assure you [he meant me] that he can speak French with the same fluency as your friend. The problem is that we are looking to the British for their support and, alas, as I understand it, the British are your enemies."

Alas, Senator Clay understood correctly. Still, he was very much the gentleman in his rejection and I was grateful that Jacque's many unkind expletives went unnoticed by him.

The secretary who had first refused us admittance was all too eager to open the hotel-room door that we might exit. With equal passion, he closed it shut behind us.

We were halfway down the hall in the direction of the stairway, when the young man in the military uniform who had been sitting at table with the Senator came down the corridor after us. Would we join him for breakfast? Of course, we would. Or so I informed Jacques who, for the moment letting anger take the place of appetite, was all for continuing to make our way down the stairs and out of the building.

Our amiable host, a Captain Thomas Hines, (he insisted we call him Thomas) was only a year or two older than Jacque and I at best, though, as I learned later, he was already a veteran Confederate spy. His frequent smiles emerged from beneath an enviable bushy blond moustache and I occasionally touched my own while we talked as if to spur it on to matching effort.

We spoke about many things during our meal (yes, I admit to eating far more than was perhaps polite), during which somehow the Captain succeeded in learning all one could know about us, while revealing very little about himself. Jacque and I had been neighbors and playmates when we were children, had played lacrosse together while studying with the Jesuits at Brébeuf, and despite going our separate ways after we started college had somehow remained friends.

We were on our third cup of coffee, when the Captain finally revealed his true purpose in dining with us. Occasionally, I would offer a comment or raise a concern while the Captain spoke, but Jacques only continued to shovel forkful after forkful of the lavish hotel breakfast into his mouth, as if in fear he would not be seeing so much food so soon again. Just as well, for I was spared translating his thoughtless remarks.

Contrary to what the Senator had told us, Captain Tom felt that we might be of inestimable aid to the Confederate cause, aid that would surely be remembered when the war was concluded. We would not be serving in a line regiment of the Confederacy; instead, our help was needed to gather information on troop dispositions and supply lines in their Northern States. And it was not the intense and eager Jacque whose aid was required, but mine.

"You write as well as speak French?" he asked. I nodded.

"I would like you to go to New York, to act as a reporter for one of your papers. Given your efforts at McGill you should have no difficulty getting hired, particularly since you need not fuss about salary as you will be getting paid by me."

This last remark, I did not translate.

"Along with your regular reports to your newspaper, you will transmit in your letters to your friend Jacque, written in French, of course, the information we really need."

And while Jacque continued to rant and rave as we made our way back along the river from the hotel, all I could think of was that I would be doing something with my life at last, no longer a school boy doomed to discuss the works of dead poets, but a patriot doing a man's work in the service of his native land.

7

Second Thoughts

Some seven or eight months after my enlistment in the Confederate cause, I began to wonder if I hadn't enlisted on the wrong side. Though, it may seem harsh to say (even harsher to confide), we Canadiens Français are the colored persons of Canada doomed to be treated as second class citizens no matter that like the Negroes settled in the New England States we are nominally free.

In the Confederacy, the landless as well as the landed look down on the Negroes and the Catholics, their Protestant version of our Lord's teachings seemingly lacking in the ways of Christian love. For that matter, their common Protestantism—whether Baptist, Episcopalian, or Methodist, binds them together only on Sundays.

More often, apart from the members of their own church, their respect, their loyalties, are reserved for members of their own clan. Enlistees in the Confederate forces that came from different states, even from different sections of the same state, had great difficulty in working with one another. Alas, for the Confederate cause, if one is to have men fight a war, they need fight together, able to depend on the men on either side of them. Too often, the rebel troupers (though unrelenting and brave) would act as if they and they alone were at war. They were fierce fighters; put two or three members of the same family side by side and they were near invincible. But an Alabama trouper fighting on Georgia soil might just decide to walk away from his regiment, paying no mind to the changing odds on the battlefield his departure meant.

We Bas-Canadiens tend to think of the Southern States in romantic terms, its people chivalrous, unyielding defenders of tradition, like ourselves, a beleaguered minority. They are home to the Arcadian French, so cruelly displaced by the English. Surely, our loyalties lie with them. But the forced exodus of the French from Canada's Atlantic provinces took place in a long ago past. In the active present, both Michigan and Illinois, loyal to the Union, are home to large numbers of more recent French Canadian immigrants.

Of course, these were truths I learned only slowly and over the course of many months. The principal reason for this delay in my education was that my initial efforts on behalf of the Montreal Herald (under a pseudonym), Le Franco-Canadien (under my own name, Jean-Paul Mercier), and gathering intelligence for Captain Tom among the Union troops. I moved south only gradually as the progress of the War dictated.

(Not incidentally, Captain Tom had been correct. Both papers proved eager to hire me once I'd demonstrated that I was both literate and not apt to quarrel about salary. The Herald was Captain Tom's suggestion; Le Canadien was mine.)

In both the North and South, my credentials as a reporter served to keep me out of prison for the most part. Of course, they offered no protection against rifle fire and cannon balls and I'd many a close call. They also marked me as a foreigner. This made little or no difference in the Northern States where entire battalions of Italians, Irish, even Scandinavians were not uncommon. But in the South, on learning I was a Canadian, the officers as well as the men often looked at me as if I had horns like a Jew.

As for the blacks, I will be honest, their presence made me nervous. I did not understand their language; they tended to swallow their words as if not really wanting to be heard. Turning to them for help, one met only with blank stares. On one occasion, while I lay in hiding, it was a Negro who betrayed my presence to the soldiers. But I am getting well ahead of my story.

Departure

I spent a month in the happy company of Captain Tom before my departure for the Yankee States in April 1861. We went over the codes that were to be used in my letters home to Jacque and discussed what information might be safely and usefully included in my newspaper reports. I was given maps of Maryland and Virginia, the areas of greatest interest to the Captain, and I was given similar-sized maps of Bas Canada with instructions on how I might overlay one with the other so as to transform a description of a Union General's march on Richmond into a seemingly innocent discussion of Tante Helene's proposed trip from Montréal to Trois Rivière.

The train by which I traveled from Montreal to Albany on the first stage of my journey gave little indication of the troubles that lay ahead for me. As we rolled across the newly built railroad trestle that connected us with the south shore of the St. Lawrence, I felt very much as if I were going off on a picnic. All the passengers shared such a feeling, I think. Our seats were comfortable and the noise and confusion which had accompanied our departure readily forgotten.

Not everyone had been as eager as I to see me on my way. My mother, heavily under the influence of our parish priest, had felt that merely being in the United States would corrupt me. Her warnings continued, judging by the movement of her lips in prayer, even as we pulled out of the station leaving her and my father behind me on the platform. (Jacque, too, was there, but he remained hidden behind a stanchion, knowing that my family disapproved of him. A long multi-colored scarf, dangling loosely about his neck, belied his attempts at concealment.)

Though my mother knew nothing of my work for Captain Tom, still she felt that my involvement in a foreign war, if only as a reporter, meant unnecessary danger.

I think she also feared that I secretly planned to enlist. "The bishop forbids it," she cried, though I suspect she knew how little the words of a bishop meant to me at that time.

My father, though less influenced by what a priest might say, clearly shared her fears. But he would never voice these fears aloud. Raised on a farm, and coming to the city only as a married adult, he had been behind my going to the university. I know he was disappointed that I had dropped out to join in this quixotic adventure. He hugged me before I left, though. And he gave my mother an equally fierce hug as if to let me know that she would be in good hands while I was away.

Apart from Jacque, my friends at the Institut Canadien had not been at all supportive. Adrien Dessaulles, who, admittedly, could be as wearying on the subject of abolition as J'accuse with his lengthy list of obsessions, insisted that the Union cause was the only one that should, that must be embraced.

With Dessaulles, as with my father, I nodded when spoken to, but his arguments did not resonate with me. I had yet to see a black man face to face, and had no idea whether they were or were not fit to be slaves. On the other hand, I felt I'd no choice but to agree with the editor of Le Franco-Canadien:

Were the United States to prove successful in reuniting their country, then, driven by Manifest Destiny, they would soon turn their weaponry northward. Had the notorious abolitionist John Brown not declared at a meeting in Canada West that, his words, "once right-thinking English-speaking North Americans had crushed the Slavocracy of the South they should then turn to overthrowing the French Priestocracy of the North."

The New York Herald, a supporter of the party Republican that had launched the War, had argued for the annexation of Canada. "The contracted views of the people of Lower Canada will be enlarged and expanded by an infusion of the Anglo-Saxon element and the energy of the people of the free States."

No wonder Le Canadien was solid in its support of the Confederacy. "Dictatorial tyranny has its way in the person of

Lincoln," my editor had written alongside a doting biography of Jefferson Davis. My stories from the war front were expected to hew to much the same line, nor did I anticipate any difficulty in following this dictum.

The editor of the Montreal Herald had no such axe to grind. "Union, Confederacy, they're all the same. Our readers just want to see the battles, up close and personal. Think of the war the way you would a hard fought lacrosse game, the more hits and injuries, the more our readers will lap it up."

Someone less knowledgeable than I might have supposed the views of these two editors to represent not only their own personal feelings but also those of their disparate cultures. But I knew of a Shakespeare that had authored not only the history plays, (that provided the blood and guts the Herald editor sought), but the tragedies with their thoughtful interplay of conflicting motives. Macbeth, which I had studied in my freshman year, offered the best of both. In the course of reporting on the American war, I would write a new Macbeth.

The journey to Albany was interrupted only once when we stopped at the Yankee border so that the officers might examine our credentials.

Across the aisle from me, a large red-faced man had brought a great many trunks and suitcases with him. He was forced to open each one of them while the officers searched for contraband. I had no similar experience. My single battered suitcase went without inspection, while my new passport was quickly stamped after a brief examination. The officer did ask me one rather curious question. What was my race? "French?" I supposed. But he wrote down something entirely different and went on to the next person.

I ate the lunch of pork, pickles, and beer my mother had been kind enough to pack for me, glanced at, then tossed aside the pamphlets Jacque had given me, and looked out at the scenery which gradually began to be revealed as we headed further south.

First, the trees shed their coats of snow. Then, as the tracks ran between canyon walls, a stream began to poke its way through the ice until finally it turned into a raging torrent. When we left the canyon it was for higher ground stripped of all snow and dotted with patches of greenery. Above us in the trees, the buds had broken open to reveal green leaves and pale pink flowers.

From time to time, we would stop at one small town or other, good-sized towns in some instances, that one or more passengers might board the train. (I never saw anyone leave the train, but this may have been because mine was a through car.)

A short time after we left each station, a conductor would appear to take a further look at our tickets. He often wore a different uniform from the man who had last examined them, suggesting, indeed the patch on his cap proclaiming, that he worked for a rail line other than the Grand Trunk.

Once, two conductors who worked for two competing rail lines appeared side by side at my chair. That is, the two rail lines competed. The men themselves were quite friendly, suggesting they must have worked side by side for some time. Each gave way to the other with exaggerated gestures until, finally, one did take my ticket. He immediately handed it back to me, remarking to his companion that here was "another Canadian guest." The pair walked away together, chuckling.

Albany

I may have fallen asleep for a short while, but when we stopped in Albany that evening to change trains and, in my case, to spend the night, I was fully awake. I needed to be.

The first hansom driver I spoke with promised for a truly outrageous sum to take me to a first-class hotel. I wondered aloud if there might not be something in the way of a second-or even a third-class establishment in town that my employer could be expected to reimburse me for. The driver, apparently satisfied that I was neither rich nor a fool, then took me to a small but comfortable boarding house nearby for half the sum I'd originally been quoted.

Meals were included in the price of the boarding house (as proved to be the case at virtually all American hostelries) and we ate supper *en famille*.

Apparently, it was the custom at dinner for all the guests to introduce themselves. All did, save for one large silent fellow with the features of an Indian, whom I learned from a second table mate was one of the construction crew working on the new State Capitol.

I was one of the last to speak, but as soon as the others learned that I was a reporter, here in the States to write about the war, virtually all of them had something more they wanted to say.

For one elderly white-haired woman, the oldest at the table, it was that she hoped that I might find something more pleasant to write about.

Her niece who sat next to her was about to say something along much the same lines, when a florid-faced man interrupted to say jokingly that he hoped the war would last long enough to have something to write about. "We'll soon have them on the run."

While no one disputed openly with this opinion, a fair-haired cleric, not much older than I, but who already had a receding hairline, volunteered that no matter how long it did take, the nation would not rest until slavery was abolished.

The young woman sitting next to him held onto his hand throughout this short speech, gazing up at him adoringly, from which I gathered, as he held her hand with equal fervor, that he must be of the Protestant persuasion and thus free to marry.

Somehow, despite my mother's fears, I didn't think the young clergyman was liable to corrupt me.

After dinner, I went up to my room, but not being tired or willing yet to attempt the bed which sagged threateningly in the middle much like a hammock, I went downstairs and out onto the porch to see what could be seen of Albany from that vantage point.

My eyes only adjusted gradually to the darkness, so that I first heard rather than saw that I was not alone.

"Not everyone shares his opinion," said a disembodied voice at my side. A slim young man with dark sideburns that partially covered his acne-pitted cheeks stood smoking a cheroot as slim as he.

"Some of us believe this war is a mistake." The young man's voice was filled with pain as if he were personally aggrieved.

Before I could learn the nature of the tragedy or tragedies that had helped form his opinion, a second voice spoke up from the step below us. "It's all about profit," the voice said in the clipped tones of a proper Englishman. I remembered the man now from the supper table, like me a relatively new arrival to the United States though a good deal older than I. "A man will have, say, an idle factory or perhaps he has made too many poorly-sewn uniforms and requires a market for them. 'Let there be war,' he'll cry to his Congressmen. And, if enough money accompanies his and others pleas to Congress, you can be sure the country will have war with its renewed demand for uniforms, weapons, and the hundred other items an army needs to go on the march."

"And never mind the poor bugger who dies in War's name. We all know who that will be." the young man interjected. Whereupon, having said all he felt could be said on the subject, the young man opened the door to the house, stepped inside and left us alone on the porch.

The smoke from a still stronger smelling cigar heralded the second man's advance across the porch toward me. "As there is to be a war," he confided, "and nothing can be done to stop that, the best a prudent man can do is to be sure he is one of the buggers who profits from it."

I forbear from any reply feeling sure that the man had only just launched into what would and did prove to be a lengthy peroration on the subject.

"Not owning a factory, nor being close friends with the President or one of his advisors, not all lines is open to us, uniforms for one. Still there is much a soldier will need of equipment that will not be otherwise available to him."

He paused, no doubt expecting some kind of brief response on my part, but I only continued to peer at him through the darkness and cigar smoke.

"Rum for one. Or whiskey, rather, as whiskey is what they drink out here in the colonies. The enlisted man always wants his drink and when he can't get it officially—damn to all those who hold the government's contracts—he'll do his best to get it unofficially. That's where we come in."

It took me a moment to realize I'd been asked to join, no, incorporated in this quixotic financial venture. My reaction much have shown on my face, for he added quickly, "T'will take only a few dollars to get started. We'll use the profits to buy more whiskey and double our money in no time."

Twice nothing is nothing, I thought, but what I said to him, gesturing toward the house behind us, was, "If I had those few dollars, do you think I would stay in such a place as this."

A moment passed in which I had time to realize how unnecessarily cruel my reply had been. If this poor man had those few dollars, would he also have elected to lodge here?

The Other Side of the River

My rooming house bed proved to be just as saggy and uncomfortable as my initial glance had first suggested. Nonetheless, I fell asleep almost as soon as my head hit the pillow and slept well beyond the hour when I'd planned to rise.

No time to prepare copy for my papers; this would have to be done on the train; though I didn't yet really have all that much to write about.

Besides breakfast was waiting. Or rather it had waited for me. A surly landlady handed me a plate of cold eggs and bacon from the oven; but to give her credit, she made a fresh stack of toasted bread, adding to it till I'd had my fill.

Walking though the capital I saw no signs of the war to come, unless it was the many flags on display. The only men in uniform stood behind the ticket window in the train station. "I need to go to New York," I said.

"Which route?"

"I didn't know I had a choice."

"Course you do," interjected a second official standing close at the first man's side, "Direct or via New Jersey. Depends on which side of the river you want to end up on."

"I want to go to New York."

"Direct is best then but can't always be counted on."

"Then I'll go the other way to Jersey."

"Direct is cheaper."

"Oh, leave the boy alone," said the other man. "Direct's not that much cheaper. What's two bits these days?"

"A plate of eggs and ham, a pot of coffee, a haircut and a shave."

"Still, tell him the truth."

I rather hoped they would tell me the truth. Or, at least, that they would sell me some kind of ticket quickly, lest I had to spend another night in Albany.

"Direct train's not running today. Line's being used by the Army."

"A ticket to New Jersey then. Please."

The second man pushed the first aside and hollered through the small window. "You'll be happier. Great view of the city from New Jersey."

"City is always best at a distance," the first man said and they both laughed.

They looked suspiciously at the coins I offered but after some further consultation with the books their trade was based on, they sold me the ticket. And just in time. I'd no sooner stepped out on the platform then the train to New Jersey, New York arrived.

New York City

The town in New Jersey in which I found myself that night was bare of hostelries. The lodging I located, finally, and only well after dark, was in the home of a family that had decided, reluctantly, to take in a lodger. The ceiling of the attic room they'd settled on for that purpose sloped in both directions and I could not quite stand erect even at its center.

"You're a tall one, aren't you? Well, you said it was for just the one night."

They'd furnished the room with a few lithographs on the sloping walls, a washbasin, a chamber pot, and a mug of hot water the landlord brought up after I was settled. I had a kerosene lamp to undress by. Once lit, I saw that my bed for the night had been covered with a multi-colored patchwork quilt of exquisite workmanship (on which I forbore from commenting for fear the landlord, a crooked-back man with a pinched-in face and a flattened nose, would take it away). The sagging bed, as clearly all beds I would encounter while lodging with strangers would sag, had been handed down from one member of the family to the next until it was my turn.

Windows at each end of the attic brought in a pleasant breeze. Not till the next morning was I to discover that they faced east and west respectively so as to bring in the dawn's early light.

I was dressed and out of the house before anyone else was stirring. Forgoing a promised breakfast—was this day not to be the true start of my career as a journalist, I made my way the few short blocks to the banks of the Hudson River. All about me, the world no longer hinted at spring, but shouted it aloud. Though patches of snow could be seen here and there upon the grass, leaves sprouted from all the trees, and one could make out the buds of what promised to be hundreds of fragrant blooms.

The ferry was not long in coming, but a crowd of men and women were already waiting to board it. From the ferry deck, the city was

19

invisible, shielded by the tall banks of the Hudson. But once I'd climbed the long stairway on the far shore, the clamor and excitement of the largest city in America was all around me.

As Adrien Dessaulles had predicted, the sights and smells of New York were overwhelming, even for a long-time inhabitant of the grandest city in Canada. As I stood gaping, trying to get my bearings, a second ferry arrived discharging its crowd. Horse-drawn trolleys came and went in every direction, and a crowd of pedestrians did their best to shoulder me aside. I stumbled for several blocks away from the river, until I reached the Broadway.

Here, I ate some fresh-baked bread and a thin slice of overly salted ham purchased from a vendor, and began to slowly stroll southward in the direction of the ocean.

The crowds were no less dense in this direction, though better dressed on the whole. Men in top hats and frock coats stood and argued on the steps of the stock exchange. Further up the street, a dozen or more shops, their windows filled with goods, competed for my attention.

Several elegantly dressed women stood gazing fixedly at me through a shop window and it was several moments before I realized they were statues, put there to display the dresses and coats they wore and not real women at all.

Then, I saw, no heard, my first soldiers. Bugles and drums preceded the marching men, the sounds of their instruments echoing off the buildings. Then, five abreast, a contingent of men in blue came marching down the center of the road toward me. I stepped aside, but fared no better pressed against the shop windows, for a parade of urchins, their swinging arms aping the movements of the soldiers, surged along the sidewalk following the parade indifferent to those they might jostle in their path. Why were they not in school? Or, at the very least, hard at work at their apprenticeships?

I must have voiced my thoughts aloud, for the elegantly dressed older woman who stood next to me, replied, "The boys can't help it. All this excitement is much too much for them. I feel like marching, too, even at my age. "

She then asked me where I was from, saying she could tell by my accent that I must be from abroad and perhaps this explained why I was not yet in uniform. I told her I was Canadian and she said that I was the very first Canadian she had ever met and that she was very glad.

She shook my hand then, and gave me her card. "As you are my first Canadian, I can give you a special price. This goes for any of my girls." I realized then, though her card made it almost as clear, that she was in the business.

Before I could take advantage of her generous offer, the band was upon us. They played, "Yankee Doodle," and other martial airs. The crowds attempted to dance in the streets before them, but were soon pushed aside by the police. After the band came the soldiers of the Seventh Regiment of Massachusetts, their bayonets brightly glancing in the sun; their steps firm; their bearing proud and erect.

The crowd parted for the soldiery to pass, but reunited before and behind them to become a dense, solid, impenetrable mass. Fire engines were brought to the street-corners and jangled their bells. Flags were everywhere. The buildings along Broadway were themselves a decoration, so variedly beautiful is their architecture, so magnificent their proportions; but I expect the street was not often decorated as it appeared that day, packed with tier upon tier of people from sidewalk to house-roof.

As we approached the open space of the Battery, the crowd only grew denser. Yet the soldiers continue to march on through the walls of human beings, close, compact, unshrinking, as the police, like a modern Moses, parted the sea of people. The soldiers marched on under a perfect canopy of flags, gilded by the sun, the cheers rolling along beside them like the thunder of canons. They marched past buildings whose fronts were covered with flags, while above them the doors, windows, stoops, and balconies were jammed with cheering men and women. Handkerchiefs, waved by fair hands and as numerous as the forest-leaves which the winds rustle, saluted the gallant volunteers.

21

I marched as close as I could behind them as we passed an effigy labeled "Jeff Davis as he would be"—hung, and bearing the motto,

" Jeff Davis, Jeff Davis, beware of the day,

When the Seventh shall meet thee in battle array."

Other unfurled banners bore mottoes in somewhat better taste, declaring the "National Guard was for the Union," and that its members should imitate the National Guard of 1776, the year the Americans declared their independence from Britain.

Somehow, I succeeded in making my way through that vast crowd, and caught up with the rear ranks as they came finally to a halt. I soon learned that the soldiers, too, were on their way south to Washington, from where they would be dispatched as a company to wherever their generals could best make use of them.

My initial attempts at conversation with the men were not particularly successful, the result, I think, of the contempt, then as now, that many servicemen have for civilians. Finally, one man, recognizing my accent, called out to a comrade, "Hey Frenchie, here's another of your lads."

"Frenchie," proved to be George Boulanger from Trois Rivière. He spoke the bare minimum of English and was pleased as punch that he was at last able to make use of his native language in conversation. Seven or eight years older than me, and never married, with watery blue eyes and an imperfect moustache, he had come to the States on the instructions of his priest to fight for liberty. Apparently, his priest hadn't heard the latest ruling from the bishops that we French of Bas Canada were to remain aloof from this war.

Our talk continued as his company, responding to a yelled command, pushed aboard the ferry.

The sight that greeted us from the deck was of an ocean harbor alive and bustling. Recall, that Montreal's harbor still waited empty of vessels for the last of the ice to clear. Here, ships were everywhere. Some at anchor, some just entering the harbor, while a fleet of small boats moved effortlessly in and around them, more ships and boats I'm sure than could be glimpsed in any other harbor in the world.

Pushed in among George's companions, I soon found myself traveling back to the same New Jersey shore I'd left early that morning, albeit somewhat further to the south where the steep banks of the Hudson gave way to nearly flat land.

Several hundred people had congregated about the Jersey City ferry and railroad depot awaiting our arrival. Immaculately clad ladies filled the balconies that extended around the railroad depot, nearly every balcony bearing the Stars and Stripes. The depot's interior was also beautifully decorated with flags. As we neared the dock, a salute was fired and the steamer Persia dipped her colors several times.

As soon as the ferry had been made fast to the bridge, the order was given to go forward. The band struck up the Yankee anthem, the 'Star Spangled Banner,' which was nearly drowned out by the accompanying cheers from the crowd in and about the depot. As the soldiers entered the railroad depot, cheer after cheer broke forth, the ladies waving their handkerchiefs and flags. By my watch, the cheering lasted for nearly twenty minutes. Just long enough as it proved for me to compose and send a telegram.

My first attempts, in French, were much too long. "All the talk is of the war. I go now to Baltimore with new friend George Boulanger of Trois Rivière. Will write soon." I cut this down considerably, and George, looking over my shoulder, said I might get by with fewer words still if I signed it with his name rather than mine. "They'll know the message is from you, will they not?"

I got the clerk's attention, barely, for he, too, was fascinated both by the armed men and the cheering crowd, but was dismayed by what he then told me. "Message has got to be in English. Military censors you know. And you can't tell where you is going." (He'd recognized the word "Baltimore," if not the balance of the message. Either way, French was out, and the plans so carefully laid by the Captain and I in the Hotel Rasco were now drifting on the wind.)

"Tell you what you can do though," the man continued, "That your train out on the platform?"

I couldn't see through the crowd, but I supposed it was. It would be my train, that is, if I could succeed in getting aboard.

23

"Tell'm you're taking old '98 instead."

And so my first message as a spy read, "Took the 98 to Three Rivers." And was signed George Boulanger.

The men and I passed through the station finally and out onto the platform where the second of two huge locomotives was being hitched to the longest train I had ever seen.

A sergeant came up to me then and demanded, his conversation livened by a great deal of profanity, to know who I was and what I was doing delaying his troops.

"He's Frenchie's pal, leave him alone," the men around us cried. But the sergeant merely said, "Wait here," as he went off to get instructions from a superior.

I had no intention of waiting—I suspected, correctly, that this train was intended solely for the army and that civilians like myself would have to wait a day or three before we could find transportation.

Fortunately, the men of George's company felt the same way, albeit for different reasons, and they swept me along with them up into the carriage. We were all in our places, and one of George's comrades had even thrown a blue greatcoat over my shoulders by way of disguise, when a lieutenant not much older than the men he commanded entered the carriage trailed a step or two behind by the sergeant who had fetched him.

"No civilians on this train," the lieutenant proclaimed. No one said anything and the men at the far end of the car who had been engaged in a healthy debate grew deathly still.

"Fellows, you heard the Lieutenant." These words came from the sergeant.

"Let him stay, Sarge, let him stay. He's Frenchie's pal." spoke up half a dozen of the men.

"Sergeant, remove that man from the train."

"Sir, perhaps it would be best if you would take the action."

The lieutenant sighed in resignation, stepped forward, and then paused as two of the soldiers, two very large soldiers, stepped out and, turning their backs, blocked the aisle ahead of him.

"I may be needed elsewhere," the lieutenant said and vanished down the corridor in the opposite direction. The men gave a great cheer, the argument at the far of the car renewed, and the sergeant settled himself in place, pushing aside one poor soldier who was now forced to walk down the corridor with his duffel and rifle to look for another seat.

Our train numbered eighteen cars in all; some like the passenger car my friends and I pushed into were similar to the ones I'd ridden in the previous two days where we sat two abreast, with fine scenic views. But the men of the Sixth Massachusetts regiment which was to accompany George's comrades in the Seventh found themselves crammed side by side on narrow benches in windowless carriages that were normally used to carry freight. Tant pis.

The first movement of the locomotives brought out cheer after cheer from the crowd, and as the train slowly glided out from the depot, the crowd kept up their cheers and waving of flags. Several of the watching ladies were in tears, deeply affected at the scene, and one old gentleman appeared to be crying like a child.

On to Baltimore

As I saw the need to take notes, George and then the balance of his comrades soon learned I was a reporter. They had already given me valuable quotes that would serve the Herald well, but the editor of Le Canadien would not be pleased to hear. Echoing the florid-faced man who'd spoken out back at the boarding house in Albany, they declared Johnny Reb would soon be on the run, the hope being that with their mission completed, they could soon return to farms, wives and sweethearts.

As for George, it was his intent to remain in Maine, south of the border. "My brothers have taken all the good land back home." We Catholics, my own parents excepted, do tend to have large families, and the result can only be less and less farmland for each new generation. A pity, for George with his square frame and broad shoulders seemed built for life behind the plow.

When we arrived at the next great city, I assumed it was Baltimore, but no, it was Philadelphia, in the state of Pennsylvania. (The Yankees appear to have as many States as we have cities in Canada.)

A great crowd of Pennsylvanians had gathered in the station to welcome us and to see off some of their own troops. The men of the 7th were grateful for their support, but more so for the food that was soon handed up through the window. George and I ended up with an entire roast chicken to split between us.

With chicken in my stomach along with half the contents from George's flask and occasional drafts from the other flasks the men passed along from hand to hand, I soon fell asleep and so missed a view of the state of Delaware through which we also passed.

While I slept, Jacque and the Captain were doing their best to make sense of the telegram I'd sent them. "Who or what is George the Baker?" the Captain asked.

"Boulanger is a common name," Jacque replied, "I imagine he lives in Trois Rivière."

"Or comes from there," the Captain added. "And I think I know what '98 might stand for." He began to draft his own telegram and to pour over the tentative itinerary I'd left behind.

Most of the men were also sleeping as we entered the outskirts of Baltimore. The sound of musket fire woke us. We didn't need the Sergeant's voice to tell us that something was up.

"You will bring all your equipment with you when we exit the train. You will leave behind anything you would not bring into action." The men groaned, those who had brought non-critical items like a favorite blanket or a sweater sewn by a wife or girlfriend groaned the loudest. But they made no protest. Apparently, they knew their sergeant well enough to know what was debatable and what was not.

Remarkably, given the liquor we'd consumed, we exited the train in orderly fashion and I looked on as the men inspected their rifles under the Sergeant's watchful eye and refilled their canteens from the large water barrel that had been rolled along the platform.

As the Lieutenant marched toward us in the wake of several other superior officers, the Sergeant put his hand on my shoulder and said in a kindly voice, "You'd best disappear now. If you plan to go on to Washington, then you need wait till we clear the city. A French accent won't protect you from bullets."

Baltimore

In 1861, Baltimore was a city of divided loyalties. Some residents were for keeping the Union together; others believed the federalists had gone too far, that Maryland ought to join with the other Confederate States in preserving the right to determine their own destiny. (These latter were my own feelings with regard to Bas Canada.)

Baltimore was also a city with two widely separated rail stations, one serving the states to the north and one serving the country to the west and south. As soldiers arrived from the north heading to the army of the Potomac they had to cross the city to board trains heading southward.

On April 19th when the Sixth and Seventh Massachusetts Regiments arrived at the President Street depot, Confederate sympathizers blocked their transfer across the city. The troops dismounted from their train and with guns loaded and fixed bayonets they attempted to march southward. A series of horse-drawn trams bearing supplies and munitions followed slowly behind them. And in amongst the troops, clinging closely to the walls of the houses was this reporter.

From Gay to South Street, the Union soldiers who marched or, rather, ran through the town were subjected to a constant barrage.

Large paving stones were hurled into the ranks from every direction. To the surprise of those in the Massachusetts regiment with abolitionist sympathies, many of the Negroes who were standing about in the streets joined in the assault.

At Gay Street, I hid in a doorway, watching as the men I'd eaten and drunk with fired a number of shots in retaliation, though without hitting anyone, so far as I could ascertain. After firing this volley the soldiers again broke into a run. I was preparing to follow, not willing to be entirely on my own in a strange city, but another shower of stones was hurled into the ranks at Commerce Street with such force as to knock down several of the men. The order was given to George's company to halt and fire. The order had to be repeated several times, both the Sergeant and the Lieutenant shouting and cursing, before the men could be brought to a halt.

The men's training took over finally. They wheeled and fired some twenty shots, but from their having to stoop and dodge to avoid the stones, only four or five shots took effect. The marks of a greater portion of their balls were visible on the walls of the adjacent warehouses, even up to the second stories.

Four citizens of Baltimore fell, two of whom died in a few moments and the other two were carried off, supposed to be mortally wounded. The Union cause gained little from these men's deaths, for those citizens of Baltimore who till then been indifferent to either side, identified with the fallen, and in an instant had aligned themselves against the soldiers.

A woman, my mother's age, the owner of the business in whose doorway I was hiding, came out of her shop to ask why such a nice young man as me was getting involved in such a dreadful business.

I explained that I was a correspondent, a Canadian, whereupon she invited me into her shop, and offered me a cup of tea and some very nice pound cake with raisins and dried plums in it.

The Union men were driven back at that moment, so that had I had not been huddled inside the shop, I might well have been the next victim of the angry mob.

As one of the Union soldiers stopped to aim his rifle, he was struck with a stone and knocked down. As he attempted to rise, another stone struck him in the face. He pushed through the doorway of the store, crawling on hands and knees. For several moments he lay prostrate, clasping his hands and begging piteously for his life, saying that his officers had threatened him with instant death if he refused to accompany them. He said—a lie—that one half of the men had been forced to come in the same manner, and he hoped all who forced

29

others to come might be killed before they got through the city. He pleaded so hard that no further vengeance was bestowed upon him, though some of the men in the shop were for it.

I was glad he was successful in his pleas, for I recognized him; he'd been among those who shared their liquor with me on the train south; yet, as a reporter, I could not intervene on his behalf.

I can't be sure what became of this man for I left before his fate was decided. The woman who'd invited me into the shop did say that once the battle outside died down, her husband would take the man to the police station to have his wounds dressed. Still, passions raged everywhere and the couple might simply have abandoned him to the mob.

The battle had moved on down the street little more than a block when I emerged to find the balance of the day a constant repetition of what had gone before. The Union men would fire a volley scattering their attackers. Their officers would order a further advance; the men would be off running, when once again some three or four parties would issue from concealment and fire into them. Some died instantly, others crawled a few steps only to fall back awaiting capture or death. The swift and the lucky would regain their feet, and proceed on with their comrades, the whole running as fast as they could.

Somehow or other, the main body of the men made it to the southern depot with me following close behind them. A running fire was kept up by the soldiers the entire distance, the crowd continuing to hurl stones into the ranks throughout the whole line of march. Alas, neither George Boulanger nor his lieutenant was with us when the sergeant herded his men onto the Washington-bound train.

Washington

The train ride from Baltimore to Washington was not a pleasant one. I had slipped aboard along with the men in Frenchie's company. We all were too exhausted to do little more than fall back into the nearest seat when permitted to sit down.

But after an hour or so, when the men had had something to drink and some of the soup the quartermasters had brought down the aisles in carts, heads began to turn toward me in my civilian clothes and thoughts form unvoiced on lips.

Some thought me bad luck; I was Frenchie's friend, but where was Frenchie, now? Some, to the contrary, thought me their own personal good luck charm, one who'd brought them unscathed through their first exposure to enemy fire. I overheard their sergeant describe me admiringly as, "the crazy man. Didn't have a gun, walked behind us bold as you please, bullets everywhere."

And then, thankfully, their talk turned elsewhere, to narrow escapes, to a pretty woman seen blowing kisses from a balcony, to a crazed old lady who'd whacked at one man with her parasol. "Did you shoot her?" "Knocked it out of her hand, then bent it across my knee. Didn't stop her though; crazy bitch, I saw her pick it up out of the gutter, wipe off the handle with her handkerchief, then use it to whack the next man."

A family of four, a man, woman and their two daughters, who had somehow crept aboard when we stopped for water en route were asked to leave the car. Seeing, but not understanding the hate-filled faces, they left quickly, hopefully to find another, more-friendly lodging for their journey, though I doubted they would.

We pulled into Washington in the darkness some hours later and sat, unmoving, for some time. Finally, the orders came and the men stood up and filed out in orderly fashion, heading, resignedly, for their next battle. I remained where I was, hoping for the chance to sleep until the safety of daylight.

31

Surprisingly, I slept uninterrupted. When morning came and I stepped out on the platform, I saw that the car I was sleeping in had been unhitched from the engine, and that the balance of the train, save for one or two cars, had disappeared.

The federal city of Washington was crowded, not merely with troops, but with the crowds of government workers and hangers on that were a normal part of the nation's capital, their numbers doubled by the need to prepare for war.

The city was well laid out, designed for sight-seeing; buildings with impressive facades were everywhere; but I had a more immediate need: to find a place to live, quickly, where I could receive messages and spend the nights to come. The hotels were all priced well beyond my means so a rooming house it would be.

The first half-dozen I visited were already overflowing, having been partitioned again and again so that still more new arrivals might be housed. Not yet discouraged, I would bump into someone on the street who would suggest another possibility. But, invariably, the next room-for-rent sign would be taken down just as I neared the building I'd been directed to.

Among the places I tried was the Peterson Boarding House across from the soon-to-be infamous Ford's Athenaeum. The latter building was impressive, but the plays it housed were second-rate trifles that did the city of Washington little credit. I believe that we Canadians, French or English, are far more cultured.

The boarding house that finally took me in was well away from town out along the Eastern Branch of the Potomac. Here, I shared a room, two in a bed, with four other journalists. They all had been in residence for at least a week, one for several months, and thus could advise me on which taverns offered the best free lunch and the most direct routes from place to place.

Two of the men were about my age. Their chief interests apart from doing as little actual work as possible were shaping their moustaches and searching out the taverns that offered the most plentiful free lunches. (What they spent on the rather weak Yankee beer easily compensated the taverns' proprietors for the food they consumed.) The other two were a good deal older than I, and while less interested in moustaches than the first pair, were no less interested in free food and over-priced whiskey. I was sure at least one of the latter two was a fellow Confederate spy, Regardless, I did not confide in him or anyone else of the double nature of my mission, having been warned by Captain Tom of how fluid loyalties could prove to be in war.

And spies in Washington were as numerous as journalists. Perhaps because as one high-ranking Union officer was to observe caustically some months later, "these damn correspondents reveal so much in their articles concerning our troop dispositions, they might as well be spies."

Ostensibly, I was a journalist, too, whose job was to get news articles for his paper. (That I would have other uses for the same information was strictly lagniappe.) I was pleased to discover that most of my colleagues were eager and willing to share a story.

Journalists, I soon learned, are a characteristically lazy lot. If one of us happened to attend a session of Congress in which something interesting was actually said, or a bill put into law, it was expected he would return with the details for all to make use of.

I often volunteered to go into town simply for the pleasure of touring the Capital. The rear of the President's mansion, the White House, looks out upon half a mile of gardens. The building that houses the Federal Patent office on Pennsylvania Avenue is two blocks long! And the Winder Building on 7th Street, the headquarters for the generals who command Lincoln's armies, is five stories high!

The majority of news that sifted down to us from the Capital was of the sort that even casual acquaintances always seem eager to impart, part truth, part wild speculation, and usually concerned which general was currently in favor with President Lincoln and his cabinet and which was not.

One had to be careful. Many stories proved to have hardly a grain of truth in them having been planted by an agent provocateur who might be working for the Union or the Confederacy or for both.

Congressmen, too, were always willing to make a contribution, just so they could get their names in their hometown paper. Perhaps the Congressman had seen and talked with the President that morning, or perhaps he had not and was simply passing on what he thought he'd overheard someone say who had.

The ruling authorities had not learned these lessons yet. Let them receive an anonymous letter and they would immediately proceed to arrest and detain individuals who were innocent of all wrong doing while allowing all sorts of dubious persons (myself included) to roam about unmolested.

At one point, I was permitted to visit a coterie of Jewish ladies who'd been placed under guard solely due to their many family connections within the Confederacy.

A Mrs. Eugenia Landau along with her two charming daughters, Melanie and Caroline, had been removed from their fine home and thrust into two dirty, small, attic rooms, evidently where Negro servants had once lived, with no comforts of any kind. A broken stove served them for both table and washstand, while a punch bowl grew into a washbasin. Two filthy straw mattresses kept them warm, and Yankee soldiers were placed at their bedroom door to prevent their escape.

The day of my visit, a Union soldier was stationed adjacent to our table, apparently that he might overhear and report on our conversations. To my delight, Melanie, the more attractive of the two sisters, spoke to me in French, informing me that it was their custom to confer in that language throughout their meals thus frustrating the guard's purpose.

Despite the shabby nature of our surroundings, our conversation was one of the merriest. Mrs. Landau was particularly voluble, the more especially as neither she nor the listening soldiers understood much of what she was saying. Her lessons in French, what she had had of them, appeared to have been long in the past. But this only increased the laughter of her daughters who prided themselves, correctly, on their knowledge of our language. Still, it answered our

34

purposes, and whether laughed at or laughed with was not of the least consequence to the women and myself.

The tale of the imprisoned women was well received by Le Canadien, but the Herald called for more stories of daring do, "your tale of house-to-house combat in Baltimore was so very-well received."

The Herald's editor would have to wait some weeks to be satisfied. Occasioning the delay was that President's Lincoln's original conscription order had called for troops from the Northern States that would serve a mere ninety days. In many instances, this period of enlistment was close to expiring, so that soldiers came and went from the city with little being accomplished in the interim.

Most of the men in uniform appeared to have had the minimum of training (I reported in a letter to Jacques) and seemed not quite accustomed to the need for military discipline. On the train from New York, the men had leaped at the sound of their sergeant's voice while ignoring the lieutenant who outranked him. Here, too, at each post I visited, while the majority of men obeyed their sergeants, they seemed oblivious to their commissioned officers and often failed to salute them.

A general sense of frustration prevailed throughout the government and the paranoia on the part of the Union authorities only grew greater, their efforts at reigning in Confederate spies more draconian and less effective.

Letters from Jacques called on me to supply him (that is, the Captain) as soon as possible with news of "our American relatives," this latter being the code-phrase agreed upon for the disposition of Union troops.

A simple request, perhaps, but one quite difficult to fulfill.

Fortunately, I soon found a way of granting it. One of my colleagues, the roommate who I was sure was a Confederate spy, brought us news of the Professor and offered to take me to see him.

The Professor was so called because of his knowledge of aerodynamics. We first heard rather than saw the man at work, when an enormous silk-covered balloon passed over our heads, preceded by the hiss of its coke-fired heater. A moment later the Professor had gotten control of his aircraft and brought its slowly back down to rest in a nearby field.

In an instant, a crowd of street urchins, both white and black, surrounded the balloon and we joined the Professor's assistant in doing our best to keep them at bay.

After turning off the heater and setting a guard over the balloon, the Professor walked quickly away, wishing to avoid all potential questioners including us. Regardless, we followed after.

"I'd like to help." I said when I caught up to him.

"Help how?" Professor Lowe looked at me wearily. Apparently, he'd heard such promises before.

"I don't know. What do you need done?"

"You could help me paint the balloon."

Later, after I'd spent some days applying a special protective seal to the balloon's fabric with a paint brush, helped him load the basket, balloon, and heater onto a carriage on days when the wind was wrong (absent the lift provided by the heated air, they proved to be quite heavy), and performed a dozen other minor chores, the Professor confided that most volunteers had little or no interest in his project beyond taking over the duty of piloting once the balloon was up in the air.

"I can do that myself, thank you very much."

Besides, he told me, there wasn't much to piloting a balloon besides turning up the heat when one wanted to go higher, and letting the heated air out when one wanted to descend; the wind did all the rest.

(Piloting a balloon proved not to be as simple as all that. Learning to read the winds, which flowed in different directions at different elevations, was an acquired skill requiring long practice.)

Yes, I did want to go up in the air with the Professor. I wasn't much different from any of the other volunteers in this respect. Significant was my intention to spy out the Union troop positions once I was aloft. Thus, unlike many similar "volunteers," I was willing to put in whatever effort was required to gain the Professor's trust.

Two things I had not expected. First, that Professor Lowe and his charming French wife Leontine would invite me to their Washington lodgings for a meal—a rather good one. And second, that much of my first trips toward the heavens would be spent wishing desperately to be back on the safety of the ground again.

One can't spy out troop dispositions while one's head is below the level of the basket so that one needn't look down on the spinning ground far, far below. And when I did look down, finally, on my second trip it was to realize that I'd no idea at all whether what I was looking at was near or far from Washington, as its buildings were invisible from our present position, or whose troops were encamped below.

What information I did glean about troop positions came from overhearing the Professor talk to others, particularly his wife, and this I did pass on in a letter to Jacques and the Captain. Still, I was almost as ignorant and as well informed as any resident of Washington when the day for the attack finally arrived.

The bulk of the information I was able to pass on, sometimes down to the exact numbers of Union soldiers and the route they would take in their attack, came from two sources. First, my colleagues and I had little or no difficulty in prying the information from Congressmen eager to be remembered to their constituents. A more reliable source was the troops, themselves. I bumped into Frenchie's sergeant one day and, when reminded of how I made my living, he asked if I might help him compose (and write) a letter home. Of course I said yes, and thereby was able to inform Captain Tom some weeks later of the day of the attack on the Manassas Junction and the route the Massachusetts regiment would be taking.

All reporters did their best to cultivate the troops—the higher the rank of the confident the better—but sometimes it was the recipient of a letter from a soldier, the proud father or mother of the letter writer who would supply their local newspaper with the details. One need only cut out the article and pass it on through one's contacts for the Confederate generals to be full abreast of developments in the North.

Bull Run

Though the city of Washington was clearly the starting point of the battles to come, for several months most of the action took place elsewhere. Conscription was instituted in several of the Northern States and volunteers were asked to extend their enlistments.

The city of Baltimore, through which the men of Massachusetts had had to fight their way, was brought firmly under Union control while the Confederate armies moved closer to Washington as the Capital of the Confederacy was transferred to Richmond, Virginia.

On the giant chessboard that the United States had become, Lincoln and Davis, the chief players, now brought their pieces into closer proximity. The Union armies crossed the Potomac into Virginia I reported gratefully, my residence having been within cannon shot of the area the Confederate artillery was now deprived of. A few weeks later the Confederates brought their own armies by rail to the Manassas Junction where they camped less than 30 miles from the Union's position.

Finally, the day came, that long-feared, yet much-hoped for day that sent the Grand Army of the North to do battle with the South, their cannon roaring, flags unfurled, guns bristling, music roaring, "On to Richmond," "Hang the Rebels," and "No chance for the wretches."

With the help of the Jewish ladies who were kind enough to loan me their bay and chaise, my roommates and I followed close behind. Too close, perhaps, for our nostrils were soon clogged with dust and the smell of horse manure.

Soon, we began to pity those poor wretches in Union blue who marched ahead of us. They had marched with brisk step as we headed south from Alexandria in the early morning, but these same green troops began to drag their feet as the day advanced and the sun rose higher in the sky. The singing had long since stopped and the men used any excuse to wander off from the main line of the march.

39

We began to pass isolated individuals sitting by the roadside, boot or boots in hand, ocher masks on their cheeks and necks from the red Virginia dust that their sweat had attracted. Once we spotted several men in uniform squatting behind a thicket drinking from their canteens. They rested there as casually as if they were at a picnic, apparently under the delusion that they could not be seen from the road.

Some of the delays were inevitable. The Confederates had blown up bridges as they fled south, and we were forced to wait while the Union pioneers placed replacement across the streams.

Soon, my friends and I grew thirsty. Fortunately, we had brought several jugs of water and some whiskey with us. We could drink whenever the desire seized us, unlike the soldiers who, barring the disobedient, must wait on command. We emptied container after container without regard to future needs, and our personal water supplies soon were exhausted.

We'd been joined that morning by a British correspondent, a William Russell. Bill, as he preferred to be called, had kept us entertained most of the day with his lively descriptions of the men around us. "Their few horses would be better off behind the plows they were unhooked from. For the best, I suppose, as their Union riders, unsuitably dressed as scarecrows, are likely to dissolve partnership with their steeds at the first sign of a gallop."

He'd been appalled by the poor marksmanship he'd witnessed. "No two guns the same. Dropping their spare ammunition whenever the weight gets too heavy for them. How do they expect to reload? Or do they think a single shot will do the trick?"

I shared with him his disgust, at least with the soldier's uniforms. How were we to report on the give and take of this giant lacrosse game if we could not tell who was playing for which team? The uniforms of the Union men were as varied as the states they came from and we could only hope the Confederates would prove more considerate of our journalistic needs.

Bill was the first to suggest that we depart from our course as so many of the Union soldiers had, and see if we might persuade one of the surrounding farmers to let us refill our canteens from his well.

"A meal will get the farmer a warm write-up in the Yonkers Tribune." added one of my roommates. "A night with one of his daughters will win him a free subscription."

Cheerful words despite our hunger and thirst. Still, a voice in the back of my head kept saying, "Cheerful though you may be on Day One of this war; what will you be like on Day 100?"

We did locate a generous farmer, finally, generous in that he gave us water freely, but we paid him for two scrawny roast chickens and some potatoes and carrots to go with them.

The drab creature with rotten teeth that served us aroused no interest in my fellow journalists and I, and soon we were back on the road. The line of armed men was still moving, though it was now close to dark, and continued to do so till only a few hours before dawn. We were weary enough when we finally stopped, albeit that we four journalists had taken turns sleeping in the carriage. How much more exhausted must those poor soldiers have been when they were finally allowed to slip their traces and bivouac, unfed, where they lay.

By the end of the second day, little further progress by the Union army appeared to have been made. What we did see was discouraging: the Village of German Town burned to the ground by Union soldiers and its farm animals butchered for no apparent reason. (It is one thing to supplement one's diet with chicken, pork, or beef; after all, this is the purpose for which these animals are raised; but the thought of wanton killing turns my stomach even today.) What right did these men of the North have to ruin another man's property merely because it lay on the other side of an arbitrary line that divided a nation?

At any rate, some of us were for turning back. Bill Russell had already left us, "No copy here. No coffee or tea either," he'd added with a laugh and gone off in pursuit of General McDowell with whom he'd apparently made friends.

41

What saved us from missing a great story was a decision by one of my colleagues, the Hartford Tribune's reporter, to find our own general. And so we began to ride here and there asking after General Tyler who was from Hartford, Connecticut, too.

Of course, Tyler was also on the move and when we caught up with him finally it was to find ourselves directly under fire, myself for the second time, counting Baltimore, my colleagues for the first.

We were not alone long at Blackburn's Ford, where the General had just ordered a reconnaissance in force. The sound of the Union's cannons, echoed in the response of the Confederate artillery from across the stream, could be heard as far away as Centerville, where the main body of the Union forces was located. Journalists by the dozens drove to the Ford from Centerville, followed rather than preceded by the less-than-eager Union reinforcements.

We found ourselves shelter from the battle, or so we fancied, amid a grove of fruit-filled cherry trees. From this hiding place, next to the slow-moving brown water, we could hear the cheers and yells of the Southern Rebels on the other side of the stream and the Union infantry's answering taunts. An instant later, a cannon ball struck a branch overhead raining juice, leaves, twigs, and bits of cherry down upon us. Fortunately, our only casualty was a splinter-filled fingertip; the correspondent from the New York Herald had been in the act of reaching upward for a ripe cherry when the cannonball arrived.

All for the best, I thought. This was the same correspondent who had argued for the annexation of Canada, observing a month before in his Herald column, "The contracted views of the people of Lower Canada will be enlarged and expanded by an infusion of the Anglo-Saxon element and the energy of the people of the free States."

The Union forces hadn't been quite so lucky, for as we retreated through the trees we stumbled upon more than one dead body. Yet, not once did we see a member of the Confederate forces. All these casualties, and Johnny Reb's, too, had come at a distance, the product of cannonballs fired at an unseen foe.

Much later, when I discussed what I'd seen with Bill Russell, he remarked on how calm we unarmed journalists had been compared with the troops themselves. "They ran every which way like frightened sheep. It was as if they'd never envisioned their own deaths, only those of a hated and unknown foe not much different from themselves."

Indeed, we had seen many soldiers running in retreat, while others were picking blueberries, seemingly indifferent to the carnage around them and their own responsibilities.

Chastened by our experience, we returned to Washington that evening in order that we might write our columns and earn our pay. (No one spoke aloud of our hidden reason for our departure, that we might not get shot at, destroyed by an enemy we could not see.)

The following day, Sunday, no mere reconnaissance in force, the entire Union army advanced across a broad front, south from Centerville toward the Manassas Junction.

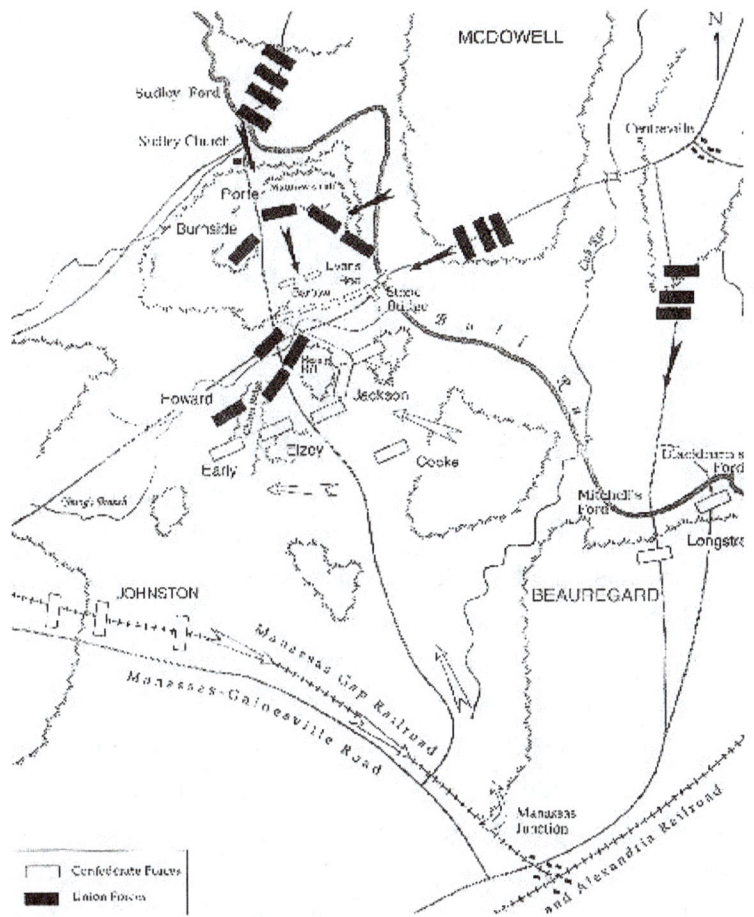

By then, the Confederate spy network had given many a forewarning of the Union intentions. The well-drilled and seasoned Confederate troops had taken advantage of the delay to bring an entire division from the Shenandoah Valley by rail; they advanced to meet the Union armies, all hope of surprise having been lost.

Even the public was aware of the Union's plans. On the day of the battle, carriages filled with spectators eager to see the Confederate defeat flocked from Washington to the battle site.

I allowed my roommates to borrow the chaise as I intended to join the Professor aloft. He'd been asked, months after his repeated offers of help had been politely but firmly rejected by the government, to aid the Army Department in pinpointing the positions of the Confederate troops about Manassas.

My fear of heights was well under control by that time and I went about the business of stowing the tie ropes without giving any extended thought to our passage upwards. With this task completed, I gradually eased myself over to the edge of the basket, almost, but not quite standing in a full upright position.

We had reached the height most favorable to a southwest passage and began a slow drift in that direction. Below us, a large mass of men in blue uniforms, at least a division in size, appeared to be moving toward rather than away from us. Later, we were to learn that McDowell had dispatched Brig. General Theodore Runyon with 5,000 troops to protect the Union army's rear.

Nobody had thought to let this General know about our reconnaissance flight and only slowly did it dawn on us that the stinging of insects all about the balloon and basket was actually the result of rifle fire from below.

Quickly, the professor turned up the heater and we rose higher and out of rifle range, or so we hoped. Unfortunately, this also meant we were drifting in a new direction, westward toward the Shenandoah Valley, rather than South toward Manassas and Bull Run.

Again, we saw troops, though this time clothed in Confederate gray. Again, they saw us. Though only the occasional shot reached our current height, these shots were enough to discourage the Professor. We changed elevations once more, and caught a new, though far less powerful wind. After what seemed far too long a period of time, we drifted back across the Potomac and passing over the District of Columbia were able finally to descend.

The morning thus wasted, I left for the scene of the battle several hours in the wake of the other journalists and did so, most uncomfortably, on the back of a horse instead of in a proper carriage.

Backside aching, I arrived at the headquarters of a Rhode Island regiment just in time to hear the drums beat assembly. A short time later, the men were on the march for Bull Run, fully aware that the enemy was waiting to receive them, yet seemingly undeterred by the prospect. I followed on horseback, but was soon forced to descend and continue on foot as the fields gave way to thick woods.

Having to lead the horse slowed me down, of course. My problem was soon resolved when a pair of soldiers at the rear of the regiment turned in their march, their rifles pointing directly at me, and "suggested" I give them my horse. A moment later, they were both astride it hightailing back toward Washington. With any luck, which I hadn't had so far that morning, they would be caught and hung as deserters.

I'd no sooner caught up with the still advancing troops then rifle shots could be heard ahead as the Union pickets exchanged fire with a group of Confederates. The main body of the Union regiment, unaware of what lay ahead for them, advanced double quick time to support their pickets yelling like so many devils.

On our arrival into the open field ahead, I judge I saw three or four hundred rebels retreating into a dense wood, firing as they retreated. From another part of the woods, a perfect hailstorm of bullets, round shot and shell was poured upon us, tearing through the ranks and scattering death and confusion everywhere. This regiment's only cowards had departed with my horse, for rather than retreat, the Union soldiers charged upon the Confederates with a yell and a roar driving them again into the woods, though with fearful losses on both sides.

We had reached the stream by this time and all took the opportunity using their forage caps, or kepi as some called them, to ladle the cool waters over their heads and shoulders and to refill their canteens.

A Union battery pulled up in support shortly thereafter and, as had been the case at Blackburn Ford, commenced to hurl destruction amid the rebels. While the men I marched with wore blue flannel shirts and gray pants mostly, the artillery appeared a regular circus in their Zouave uniforms with its embroidered jacket, baggy trousers, sash and Egyptian fez.

But we did not have much time to pause in admiration. The Confederates came charging upon the battery from another quarter and the orders were given for the men to fall back and protect it. Only a fraction of the original regiment was in the fight, the others having lagged too far behind. While the men were preparing to make a final effort to keep the battery out of Confederate hands, (and, not incidentally, keep this reporter alive), the 1st Rhode Island regiment came filing over the fence and poured a volley out to the Secesseh that drove them under cover again.

The 1st Rhode Island was followed by the New York 71st and the Hampshire 2nd regiments. Our group was allowed to fall back and I took the opportunity to go with them. The last I saw of the action was a bombshell strike a man in the breast and literally tear him to pieces. He was not alone in death. The groans of the wounded and dying were audible everywhere.

Later, I descended the hill to the woods that had been occupied by the rebels; here the bodies of the dead and dying were three and four deep, and not just whole bodies but parts as in an animal abattoir. Intestines hung like confetti from low bushes, and were one fool enough to look upon a corpse, one might see soldiers with no faces or with holes blasted completely through them.

The shots flying pretty lively round me by this time, I thought it best to rejoin the retreating regiment once more. I gained the top of the hill just as the sound of our batteries gave out, they not having but 130 shots for each gun during the whole engagement. This left the brigade with nothing but infantry to fight against the Confederate batteries—the Union cavalry were not of much use because the rebels would not come out of the woods, and the command was given to retreat.

What remained of the Rhode Island 1st and 2nd regiments, plus the New York 71st and the New Hampshire 2nd were drawn into a line to cover the retreat, but when an officer galloped wildly into the column crying the enemy is upon us, off they started like a flock of sheep with every man for himself and devil take the hindmost. The rebels' shot and shell fell like rain amid the exhausted troops.

As we gained the cover of the woods the stampede became even more frightful. The baggage wagons and ambulances became entangled with the artillery and rendered the scene more dreadful than the battle, while the plunging of the horses broke the lines of the

Union infantry, and rendered any successful formation out of the question.

The rebels, themselves being so badly cut up, may have supposed we had gone beyond the woods to form for a fresh attack. Rather than advance, they proceeded to shell the woods for a full two hours, whereas if they had begun an immediate attack, nothing in heaven's name could have saved us.

The rebels opened a very destructive fire upon the Union troops as we neared the bridge, mowing down the men around me like grass, causing even greater confusion than before. The Union artillery and baggage wagons became fouled with each other, completely blocking the bridge, while the bomb shells bursting on the bridge made it rather unhealthy to be around. As I crossed on my hands and knees, a Captain of the Second Regiment crossing by my side was struck by a round shot and completely cut in two.

I did not belong on a battlefield, I realized belatedly. Once across the bridge, I started up the hill as fast as my legs could carry me— wishing every moment that I was still astride my horse—and passed through Centreville and on to Fairfax.

I returned to Washington that night surrounded by men who like me were more dead than alive, having been on their feet 36 hours without a mouthful to eat, and having traveled a distance of 40 miles with at most a twenty-minute halt.

The last five miles of our march were perfect misery, none of us having scarcely strength to put one foot before the other. The cheers we received going through the streets of Washington seemed to put new life into the men around me, for they rallied and marched briskly to their camps. Whereupon, I suppose, just as I did when I reached my boarding house, they dropped on their beds, if they had them, and, in an instant, were asleep.

After the Battle

The resultant reportage varied from intimate details of an army in action to sweeping descriptions of the engagements and strategies employed. The latter being written by those slug-a-bed correspondents who'd stayed in Washington and based their reportage entirely on what their military contacts said might have happened.

As always, the further away from the battle, the more insight the author appeared to have. Regardless, on the grand scale, no one really knew what had happened. The daylong action at Bull Run had occurred on a dozen or more fronts while troops advanced and retreated, sometimes in an orderly formation, and sometimes in a complete state of panic.

What I reported in clear to my papers and in code to the Captain was what I had seen and heard as I, too, retreated and advanced, sometimes on my feet, as often crawling to avoid being shot. I was sure the editors at the Herald would be pleased because of the close ups of the action I'd provided. The editor of Le Canadien and the Captain, too, would be pleased by my description of the Union troops panicking in retreat.

The Captain was already pleased with my efforts, for attached to the latest letter from "Jacque" with some unexpected instructions was a further letter of credit.

I attributed the Union's failure at Bull Run to many things including ill-trained and ill-equipped troops, and poor leadership. But most of all because, as the British gentleman at the Albany boarding house had proclaimed to all who would listen, this War was about profit. Within the space of their three-month enlistment, the ill-made shoes and uniforms of the Pennsylvania regiments had all worn through. Without pants and shoes, they had refused to attack when ordered by their commanding officers. On the plus side, at least as far as the shoe and uniform manufactures were concerned, their factories would soon be working at full capacity again as they cranked out equally defective replacements.

We civilians were all too aware of the return of the fleeing Union forces to Washington bringing with them unlimited numbers of the dead and the dying. Though we lacked any solid information, we were very much afraid that the Confederate forces soon would advance on Washington with what seemed very little standing in their way.

Less disposed to panic, though bitterly disappointed by the failures of the previous days, McDowell and the other Union Generals recognized, at last, that they needed to know more about the disposition of the Confederate troops to plan their defenses. Till that moment, the Professor was aware he'd been little thought of by the Army command; still, he pretended not to be surprised when a young Lieutenant rode up the next morning with a letter from McDowell asking if he would be kind enough to do one further ascent to obtain this information.

"I knew they'd come around."

On July 24, Prof. Lowe and I set out in the Enterprise once more. What we were to report might well mean that the war was already lost and that the rebels of the Southern States had won their independence.

We had favorable winds, were not fired upon by either Union or Confederate troops, and were able to observe the Confederates moving in and about Manassas Junction and Fairfax. We saw no evidence of massing Rebel forces and upon our return with this information we were sure all Washington would breathe a little easier. That is, they could and would if we could succeed in returning. (Captain Tom, alas, would not be quite so pleased.)

We had a problem in so doing, more than one, in fact. The winds we needed for our return were at a higher elevation, and the balloon would not go higher. "The seal's not holding." Indeed, the balloon had begun a slow descent toward the ground and by the look of things, we'd soon be landing in enemy territory.

On the plus side, we succeeded in bringing the balloon down safely, just, clear of the trees, on the edge of a field. Still, we were behind Confederate lines. I helped the Professor to collapse the balloon, stow it in the basket, and then pile brush around it in a poor imitation of a haystack. It was the Professor's intention to wait and see if somehow a rescue of both he and the balloon might not be accomplished. "If the Rebs retreat and our troops advance," was how his prayers began.

My intention was to get the hell out of there as quickly as possible. I reasoned we were in for a rough time whichever group of soldiers first came upon us.

I thought I'd persuaded him, but when we started off together, he fell against me, his hand on my shoulder. "I think I twisted my ankle." Perhaps, our landing hadn't been quite as gentle as I wished to remember.

Again, I had a choice: to wait with him for possible rescue or to leave in search of help. For some moments, I sat next to him in the shelter of some bushes, but the inactivity did not serve me kindly. The very next instant I was on my feet and shaking the Professor's hand, preparing to depart.

He wished me well. I wished him likewise. I never saw him again.

The Professor would need stay the night under the stars before he was rescued and could report to headquarters. Fortunately, members of the 31st New York Volunteers found him before the enemy could. Even then, as he was not able to walk out with the troops, he had to wait while they went off to report his position. Eventually, his wife Leontine, disguised as an old hag, a far cry from the beautiful woman she actually was, came to his rescue with a buckboard and canvas covers and was able to extract him and his equipment safely.

Later he would report that his observations "restored confidence" to the Union commanders.

Not all my roommates had been as fortunate, or so it seemed. The supposed confederate spy did not return, at least not immediately. Only much later, long after the war, would I learn through a chance contact that he had been a double agent, and that he'd used the opportunity of the attack on Manassas to stay behind and begin sending reports home to the Union.

51

Readers of these notes may well wonder what happened to me. Had I simply walked away to abandon the Professor? In a way, yes, I had, though it was more in the nature of an act of forgetfulness than strict abandonment. What happened was that I met Luke, a deserter from the Confederate army who was to be more or less my companion though the next six or seven months.

To the Shenandoah Valley

Ungainly as a scarecrow and dressed in as ill-fitting clothes, Luke lay with his back against a haystack, his rifle propped beside him. He made no move toward the rifle when I emerged from the woods, which endeared him to me.

"Who be you?"

"Jean-Paul. I am a journalist for Le Canadien."

"Fureigner."

"*Mais sur*. And you?"

"Kentuckyian. Thought I'd come see what this war was about. Didn't care for it."

I nodded my appreciation for his viewpoint. Nonetheless, he added, "Can't see any need for killing strangers.

"You see any troops around here?"

"I thought it best to avoid them."

"Me, too. Well, we'd best be on our way, then."

Even now, I'm not sure why I followed him. But a few moments later, we were on our way, this deserter and I, back to his home in Kentucky. I'd admitted at some point in our conversation that I had never been to this state and added, politely, that I hoped to visit it someday. But surely I'd not intended to set out for Kentucky that very afternoon.

Luke had little choice in the matter. Having discarded his Confederate uniform, he would likely be shot as a deserter by any Confederate troops we encountered or, should we first run into a Union regiment, he'd be shot as a Confederate spy.

He didn't seem to have thought ahead. Indeed, planning was not in Luke's nature judging by the haste with which he'd left to join the War and the equal rapidity with which he'd chosen to abandon it.

I asked him at one time if he or his family had slaves and he only laughed in response. When we came eventually to his small family farm, I saw the source of his laughter, for the homestead was located on a hillside that was as much rock as arable soil. Luke, his parents, and his brothers did their best to stay the course from year to year. The hunting rifle Luke carried had been the chief source of meat for his family, chickens being kept for their eggs, and a single cow for its milk. "Ain't no plantation, that's for sure."

Luke didn't like the men who owned plantations, hadn't liked them giving him orders during his brief army career. "They ain't no better'n me."

I wonder if he would have done better in a Union regiment whose officers were elected. Probably not.

Our first day on the road passed slowly, as we need move with great caution to avoid all troops. Still, by nightfall, we had crossed the Rappahannock and spent the night near Culpepper in a barn on a seemingly abandoned farm.

We moved that first day as if still at war, and liable to be shot at any moment. We kept ourselves hidden as much as possible; staying when we could in the shadow of trees, outbuildings, haystacks, and whatever other cover was available.

Now, we felt able to move with greater freedom, in the quite possibly unjustified belief that we'd left all the armies of both sides far behind. The result was that we were seen more often by civilians, usually just women and children as their men folk had either volunteered or been pressed into service.

They scowled at us for the most part and had a child not given voice to their thoughts we might have gone hungry and thirsty the entire day. "Cowards," he hollered, before his mother, or perhaps it was his older sister, succeeded in schussing him.

"They think we're deserters," I said to Luke.

"But we are," he replied, "at least I am." A reply that indicated that however good his instincts might be—he had kept us fed and out of harm's way that first day and was to do so successfully for the most part in the days that followed—his thought processes were second rate at best.

Coming across a set of laundry hanging out to dry, I ripped a sheet off the line and tore off strips with which to bandage his arm and my leg. These bandages were too clean for what I had in mind, but a little dust from the road soon fixed that and the false bandages labeled us not as deserters but as wounded war veterans.

The happy result was that suspicion gave way to sympathy and even hospitality as those who fed us hoped others would care for their absent loved ones in turn. We ate well that day and that evening joined a mother, daughter, and grandfather at table, it no longer being necessary to steal corn from a field or half-ripe apples from a tree.

The once-comely mother had an attractive face, but her arms and hands were already showing the effect of too much hard labor merely to keep her family alive while her husband was gone. The grandfather clearly did what he could on the farm, but he moved slowly and I imagine it took him three days to do what the woman's husband had formerly done in one. The woman's daughter, too, did her best to be helpful, but there are limits to the efforts of a small child.

When man fights man on a grand scale and entire armies do their best to kill and maim the masses of men opposite them, it is easy to forget that the vast number of conflicts, petty though these may be, arise between neighbors. The small farm we spent the night on and the huge plantation next door shared a stream as a common border. The two farmers had always had an equitable arrangement for the stream, having more or less grown up together, though the one was rich and the other poor. Now that both were away, our hostess' husband a sergeant in the regiment the other served as captain, the always-present animosities between the women of the two houses had come to dominate the families' relationship.

"They've darkies, and we've none; that's always the way its been," explained the grandfather as he led us to the barn where we would spend the night. "Their plantation is large enough that they've always been able to afford to pay a man to oversee the field hands. I never liked that man. The instant Tom, our William's friend, was gone, his wife took the man into her bed, twisted leg and all.

"Now, he thinks he's the boss. And their two boys, big hulking brutes both of them despite their young age, follow him about as if they were puppies.

"He wants our land. Had his darkies put up a fence on our side of the stream. Wants to keep us away from the water."

"So, you shoot him." Luke said, stating what for him was the obvious.

"And he'll shoot back and then where will Becky be with no man at all to care for her."

Seemed reasonable to me and I thought no more about it as I fell asleep. Early the next morning though, barely dawn, Luke shook me awake and told me to follow him.

"Breakfast," I suggested. But he just motioned again for me to follow and, rifle in hand, started off across the field away from the house where we'd eaten the previous evening.

A few moments later, we were at the fence we'd heard about the night before. Rather than go around, Luke pulled up on one of the fence posts and waggled it back and forth like a tooth until he'd loosened it enough to yank it part way out of the ground. He signaled for me to help him then and together we stepped on the adjoining fence line until the post ripped free of the earth and we could step over and onto the fence and ford the shallow stream.

We walked then for a quarter of an hour through fields of corn until we came in sight of a large house and a series of outbuildings. Smoke was issuing from the chimney of the house and I wondered what Luke thought he was up to. From what we'd heard the night before, the people who lived here didn't strike me as the sort likely to offer hospitality to travelers even ones pretending to be wounded war veterans.

They had to know we were coming; dogs were barking, and the occasional dark face could be seen peeking out a window. But Luke, as certain as if he were on his own property, kept walking straight toward the buildings.

An elderly colored man was leading two already-saddled horses out from the stable. Luke veered in that direction and I followed him. He held his rifle in such a way that it could easily be pointed at the colored man. The man seemed well aware of this.

"Who them horses for?" Luke asked.

"The young masters."

"Take'm back inside the barn."

"Now," Luke added when the man did not move and raised the rifle.

The man hobbled back into the stable.

"How many more horses?" Luke asked once we were inside. The stable was a long one and could easily have held as many as ten or more horses in its stalls.

"Four. Only one's fit for riding though."

"Bring it out." The man rushed to do so, though rushing seemed only to make his movements more awkward.

"Get on," Luke said to me and pointed to the smaller of the two already-saddled horses. When I hesitated, he practically shoved me in its direction, and when I hesitated again, one foot in the stirrup, he gave me a boost up.

The other horse was out of its stall now, and Luke took the reins from the man. "You go sit on that bale of hay," he said to him. Then he swung himself up in the saddle as if he'd been born to ride, and leading the other horse behind him, started out of the barn.

I followed. What we were doing made as little sense to me as any other part of our adventure, so why not follow. The yard was now crowded with people, all of them darkies. Most were clustered around the steps of the big house. A white man emerged from the kitchen door; though he had one withered leg, he was bear-like in stature with arms as thick as fence posts. In one hand, he carried a whip. "You stop right there!" he said, and started toward us, his game leg dragging behind the other one.

Two boys emerged from the house at this moment still half-asleep and dressed in their nightclothes. "Stop'm," the men cried and one of the boys dashed toward us. Luke simply leaned forward, nudged his horse sharply with his heels and started off in the opposite direction. Both the other horses followed with me doing my best to hold on to mine. The boy and some of the darkies may have chased after us but I was too busy concentrating on staying in the saddle to look back.

Luke was sensible enough to let the horses find their own path and soon we were on our way out of the area, though in a more northerly direction than Luke desired. We corrected our course at a crossroads and started off again heading southwest, the ridge of mountains still on our left, the sun now well above the horizon to our right.

We continued at the fastest pace the horses were content with for some time, stopping only when we needed to ford another stream in order that the horses might drink.

I pointed out to Luke that I could use a drink myself as well as the breakfast I'd talked about earlier. "Drink up then," he said and pointed to the bare-trickle that was the stream, "Breakfast I don't know about.

"Don't worry about them chasing us. We still got all their horses." He pointed to the unsaddled roan that was lapping up the shallow water as happily as the ones we'd been riding.

We bypassed the next two villages we came to, but at the third, Luke inquired at the smithy if they'd be interested in buying a horse. Remarkably, we struck a satisfactory deal, or so Luke claimed, and were now able to buy us a lunch with enough food left over to have a good supper that evening off the road and out of sight.

Blacksburg

The following day, still on horseback, we were able to cross into the Shenandoah Valley near Waynesboro largely avoiding the higher elevations of the Blue Ridge Mountains.

For the next three days, our path would be determined by a desire to avoid climbing into the hills, which now could be glimpsed, on either side of our southwest path. I still wasn't quite sure why I was traveling with Luke or where we were headed. Perhaps, like him, I'd just had enough of war for a while.

We did not make as good time as before. While long stretches of road led us amid fertile fields of green where lunch was for the picking, just as often, the path would take us up for a bit, then down again. When the footing was poor, we needed to lead our horse; at the end of the day, our calves ached from walking up and down the hills.

On the fourth day, someone stole our horses while we were sleeping.

Luke was remarkably irate for a man who was himself a horse thief. He waved his rifle about as if intent on doing harm and would have, I imagine, had the thief or thieves been stupid enough to return to the scene of their crime. Luke must have thought he was an Indian, for after making a last panicked circuit of the camp, he bent down to peer at the ground as if trying to make out in which direction the horses had been led away.

I was happy to go along with his decision that the tracks went off in the direction we'd been going originally, (though a good deal less happy that we'd be forced to proceed on foot from now on). Luke still had his rifle, so who knew what would happen if we actually caught up with the horse thieves.

Fortunately, we'd been no more than an hour on the road, a cold breakfast inside us, when an elderly farmer driving a wagon laden with produce invited us to join him. His team of equally elderly mares looked back at us as if this was a bit more than they had bargained for, but they stepped forward nonetheless with their new load, albeit moving not much faster than we'd been traveling on foot.

We had to walk alongside the wagon on some of the uphill portions, but we were used to that. Besides, the farmer let us try a couple of his tomatoes, and a little knife work gave us access to the firm flesh of several tasty cucumbers.

The trip through rolling farm country would have been a quite pleasant one, despite the slow pace, had it not been for the aroma of manure that came from the farmer and, though I can't be sure of this, ourselves.

We had barely entered the market town of Blacksburg where the farmer said he expected to get the best prices for his load, when we were stopped by a small group of Confederate soldiers. They were a press gang as it turns out, immaculately dressed in pressed uniforms that were a far cry from the torn and tattered remnants that clothed the survivors of Bull Run. They took one look at Luke and me and decided that here was ideal material for the Confederate army.

"Step down from the wagon," commanded their officer; and, in the face of the many drawn rifles, we proceeded to do so immediately.

"You boys want to serve your country?"

One of the soldiers snickered. His officer immediately gave him a harsh look that shut him up.

I saw it was up to me to save us from this situation. Speaking in French and showing my credentials as a correspondent might save us, me anyway, if the officer also spoke French, that is. I couldn't get away with much fast-talking if he didn't. Fortunately, I had a better idea.

I'd been part of a group in my freshman year at McGill that performed Shakespeare's Henry the Fifth. Though I can speak as flawless English as the best of England's actors, the part they'd assigned their token French-Canadian was that of Katherine, the French King's daughter and Henry's betrothed. If I could just rid myself of the falsetto I'd adopted for the part, then I could speak a sort of corrupted English to the officer that would immediately brand me as a foreigner yet allow me to be understood.

The ruse worked, though the officer stood for a long time, gazing at my papers. The Union forces had issued them after all.

"You can go," he said, finally, and pointed off in the direction of the town before turning to Luke. "Swear this man in."

"But he is one of you already," I said in my bad English, "a prisoner of war who was assigned to escort me to the Kentucky."

"Oh, yes? What regiment?"

"2nd Virginie." Luke volunteered.

The officer considered this for a moment. Apparently, Luke's accent did not ring true. I had trouble from time to time understanding him myself. "Where you from originally, soldier?"

"Kentucky, near Chatanoogie." Luke said, which was more or less what he'd told me.

"Chattanooga's in Tennessee." interrupted one of the enlisted men.

"Kentucky!" Luke persisted.

The two looked as if they might come to blows.

"I need this man," I said, hoping to keep Luke with his ready instinct for survival as a traveling companion. *"C'est très dangereux, ici."*

"Vous est Français?" asked another officer who had just ridden up to join the group. His accent was very bad but he was filled with laughter, which was exactly what the situation called for.

"Bas Canadien," I replied and then explained my presence once more.

"Let'm keep the fellow," said the new arrival, pointing to Luke. "These mountain men are near useless, any way."

"Get going then," the first officer said.

But Luke did not know when to leave well enough alone. "Them's our horses," he said, pointing first to the one the new arrival sat astride and then to the one that followed after on a lead.

"Like'm?" the officer who could speak French said. "Just bought'm. Fellow wanted $50 a piece for 'm, then tried to argue when I told him what the army was willing to pay."

"Should of just taken them, Sir." said one of the men. "We're all in it for the cause."

"The 4th Virginia!" hollered another and the men all cheered.

I took Luke by the arm; we were not going to get those horses. He followed meekly enough, happy I suppose that he still had his freedom. So we finished that day on foot just as we'd begun it.

So often Luke's behavior was proof, if further proof were needed, that idle hands make the devils handiwork.

We got away from Blacksburg as fast as we could—who knew when or whether the officer in charge of the press gang might change his mind. Fortunately the way out of town led past the farmer's market and we picked up a goodly store of grub to carry with us. The same road led past a couple of taverns, also. But with the threat of the press gang reinforcing my pleas, I was able to persuade Luke that stopping might not be in his best interest.

We didn't reach Kentucky that first evening or the second, and we weren't offered a ride either. With rain clouds beginning to gather overhead, and the soles of my boots near worn though, I was beginning to regret the entire trip.

We stopped on the edge of a field to rest and I'd closed my eyes for just a few seconds when I noticed Luke was missing. I'd been thinking of some questions I would like to ask him, though I knew I'd no hope at all of getting any sort of useful answer in response.

While I might be curious as to why he did what he did in the way he did it, he was not one for thinking deeply about things and seemingly lacked all curiosity as to motives or intentions. A man was good or bad in Luke's view, no in between. He did what he did because he did it; that was all.

Luke was not much for talking either, though occasionally he would voice his thoughts aloud like a small child. He was quick to point out a pock marked apple in which a man's face might be discerned or a cluster of branches that might be taken at a distance for the steeple of a church.

Sometimes his thoughts on such subjects would come seemingly from nowhere: Did I remember the man with the squashed face, nose no larger than that of a pig, that we'd seen on the streets of Blacksburg the day before?

He would remark on the resemblance of a certain cloud to a bird, yet never would ask as I did when we encountered a new feathered friend in our travels, like the bright orange one with a long black tail perched at that moment on a nearby fencepost staring down at me, what kind of bird it was.

Most of all I wanted to ask him why, if life in the Kentucky hills was as hard and unrewarding as he said it was, he so wanted to return. How could one live in a place without architecture, without theater, without music?

The answer came to me much later, after I'd spent two winters in the States, winters so much milder than the fierce unyielding cold that possesses Bas Canada for six months of the year. I found so much in the Southern States—Virginia, Kentucky, Mississippi, Louisiana, Georgia, and South Carolina that was beautiful. Yet, when the opportunity arose a year or so later for me to return home to that unyielding cold I seized on it.

Compared to the land we walked through that morning, Bas Canada is barren, its trees stunted, its flowers and fresh fruits rare events. Yet Bas Canada was where I lived, Bas Canada was home. In the end, we all choose to live where our homes are.

A moment after I ceased these reflections, Luke reappeared. He was leading a horse. Yes, he'd stolen another one. No saddle this time or stirrups either. I was at a loss to think how I might mount to the area on the horse's back he motioned me toward, but after getting up himself, he simply pulled me up behind him by the arm.

We took off like a rocket and I'd no choice but to hold onto him or risk breaking multiple bones. If I'd thought previous horseback rides uncomfortable, this one was equivalent to some Old-Testament prophet's bed of thorns. I was sore everywhere in minutes, but Luke had no intention of slowing down. "They may be after us," he called back over his shoulder.

I didn't ask who "they" were, nor had I the breath to do so. Thunder could be heard off in the distance and the occasional raindrop mingled with the sweat on the horse's flanks. We were making good time all right, but at what cost.

After what seemed like hours, but probably wasn't more than one, the horse began to move more slowly, thinking, I imagine, that two riders was one too many, and that a trough of water, a good rubdown, and a manger full of oats would go quite nicely at that moment.

"You hear something?" Luke asked.

I did hear something, the sound of many hoof beats following us in the distance. But before I could pass on the news, Luke had veered off into the woods on the left, leaving what passed for a road in those parts well behind.

After five minutes or so, he brought our ride to a stop, something our mount was more than eager to do.

Dismounting, and throwing the reins into the underbrush, he took off running between the trees. With somewhat less success, I tumbled off the horse into a bed of ferns and crushed leaves, and did my best to follow after. I never saw who or what was chasing us, or whether anyone was chasing us at all, which was probably just as well.

The way amongst the trees was heavy going, the underbrush lush and full. While I've no doubt some find elderberry and Phacellia blossoms attractive, the leaves of the latter are rough and clinging if you fall among them.

I'll say this for Luke, once it started to rain, he waited for me to catch up with him. Seems he wanted to brag. The horse he'd stolen had saved us a couple of hours on the march hadn't it? Never mind that we would use up more than that amount of time wandering through the woods. And with the sun no longer visible overhead, who knew what direction we were wandering in.

Fortunately, the natural inclination of someone on foot, not entirely sure of his direction, is to drift downhill. Though it took at least another half hour, by the end of which we were wet through and through, we found ourselves following a slow-moving streamed in what Luke said was sure to prove be the right direction.

When the sun broke through the clouds again, he proved to be more or less correct. And when we suddenly came upon a rowboat flipped hull side up on the bank of the stream, I realized we might have found something better than a horse or, at least, a good deal more comfortable.

Strangely, Luke was not eager to help me flip the rowboat over, and when I told him to get in, he looked at me with something akin to panic. Was this horse thief balking at stealing a rowboat?

"I can't swim." he said.

"We've forded many a stream, already."

"This is different."

I succeeded finally in persuading him to step into the part of the boat that was still on the bank, after which I pushed the craft into the stream and wadded out into the water to get on board myself. (I was already wet, so what difference would it make? I did take my boots off and put them in the boat before I pushed out into the stream.)

A child's voice from the bank behind us halted me half in and half out of the boat. "You going to the circus? Can I come with you?"

The young towhead—he couldn't have been more than eight or nine—did seem eager to join us, if we were going to the circus, that is.

"Best ask your mama first," Luke said.

"I don't think she'll let me go." the boy confided.

"We can't take you with us then."

"Still, I could ask her."

We promised to wait for him, but like so many of the things adults promise children, it was not to be. We were already out and moving in the swift moving current, when the boy's mother and maybe a shotgun-bearing father and uncle came down to the bank of the stream to see who was messing with their boat.

Had it still been raining, the trip down the Pelisipi might not have been quite so pleasant, but it took only a modest amount of effort to keep the boat centered in the stream and the current did all the rest. An unending series of variegated ferns and flowers grew beneath the alders and aspen we passed on the banks and thus the trip was far from boring.

Every so often an enormous chestnut tree would be seen towering above the otherwise straggly growth. We stopped once where an orchard grew close to the stream. I was stepping out on the bank to get us some fruit when I noticed that Luke was sitting petrified at the far end of the boat. "I'll be right back."

Luke's lips registered a protest but no words came out. Clearly, he was afraid the boat would drift away downstream once I left and take him with it. Contenting myself with a single peach hanging within arms reach from a limb that extended out over the bank, I sat back down again.

The peach had been delicious. "Too bad about the kid and the circus," I said, hoping to change the course of his thoughts when I saw he was still sitting in the back of the boat petrified gripping the edges of his seat.

"They never took me," he said. "They promised though, many times.

"You ever bin to a circus?"

I told him I had and didn't mention that I'd sort of outgrown it. "Starts with a big parade into the center ring, the camels, the horses, with a beautiful lady riding bareback on each one, and then the elephant."

I'd started to tell him about the origins of the circus in Roman times when he found his voice again.

"I always wanted to be in the circus, maybe be one of those wild west riders, like Jeb Stuart and his cavalry. 'Course we didn't have a horse. Only one we borreyed sometime from my Uncle when we wanted to open up some land. When they caught me trying to ride it, they tanned my britches."

This memory seemed to have relaxed him, for he soon overcame his apprehensions and let his fingertips trail in the stream. At least, he did until a fish nibbled at his fingertips. He drew his hand back then as if he'd been stung, while I did my best not to laugh.

"T'aint funny."

But it was funny and the warm sun soon dried our clothes. We probably made 40 miles that day, though as streams tend to switch back and forth like the path of a snake crossing a road, we probably traveled a good deal less as the crow flies.

Fever

I've very little recollection of the next few days. I recall waking up stiff and sore and shivering the morning after we stole the boat, though this last is not uncommon when one is forced to sleep outdoors. The dampness near the river where we'd spent that night only exacerbated the chill.

Luke was dead set against a further boat ride—so much for my belief that he would grow to like the feeling of freedom one had riding the current. We headed inland instead toward the mountains and the road we'd left the day before.

I'm sure we had to cross someone's farm; we may even have stopped there for a welcome hot meal—I remember an apple orchard, but after that things began to blur. I was being hauled along—"Just a few more steps."—and then I was on the back of a horse. Or was I riding in a wagon? I was resting on a mattress made of corn shucks; someone was giving me water; I needed water, it was so very hot.

And then—it was more than a week later, I woke atop a straw mattress to see a glasses-wearing young girl with a chipped tooth looking down on me. Her glasses were thick as silver dollars and tape held one of the side frames in place.

"I'm fourteen years old," she said apropos of nothing at all. "These are my aunt's glasses." She held them out to me. "Harder to see with them, than without." She blinked several times, and then moved her chair closer so that her face sans glasses was very close to mine. "You're awake, huh."

"Who were those people?" I asked Luke later.

"They weren't exactly kin. Same good people, though. I more or less told them I'd fought alongside their son in the war."

"You lied to them."

"They took care of us, didn't they? I told them their son died in my arms. They was mighty broke up about it.

"Don't look at me like that. He probably did die. Most of us did; most of us will."

And how I wondered, though I did not say this aloud, did you explain how you were here with me when other men were dying at the War?

The girl said, "You're cute, a might thin though. I'm goin' to feed you, fatten you up.

"Most of the boys round here, the men too, are stupid heads. Your friend [I assume she meant Luke] is a stupid head too, but my sister likes him."

I was to learn that Luke had not only charmed the mother and older relatives of his imaginary comrade, but he'd charmed the pants off the oldest daughter, and had spent a pleasant week with the family while I lay in bed with the fever.

"I've got an education," the girl said, and pointed about her. The narrow shed not only held tools and my straw pallet, but perched on homemade bookshelves the eighth edition of the Encyclopedia Britannica sat in solitary splendor.

"I know all about Coleridge and Cristobel and opium and everything."

How had such a thing as the eighth edition only recently arrived on the bookshelves of McGill made its way here into the hills of Kentucky?

But before I could discuss this with the skinny awkward teenager with the chipped tooth and her aunt's glasses, Luke and a buxom version of the girl before me came into the room.

"Rachel, you go fetch this man some breakfast," the new girl said, skipping the amenities.

"Cristobel, you call me Cristobel," the skinny girl called out as she vacated her chair.

"I'll whip your backside." Still holding Luke's hand, the dominatrix turned then to me. "You need to go?" she asked in her best imitation of Florence Nightingale.

I thought maybe I did.

"Kin you walk?" Luke asked.

69

I grunted a maybe and stood. Dizzy, I sat down again.

"Give him the bedpan," the older girl said disgustedly and stalked from the room.

I did get up by myself later that day and I did eat all the breakfast, every bite of it that Rachel brought to me. Rachel and Luke both came to see me many times that day, though Luke often was compelled to leave at the sound of his mistress' shrill voice. The officers he'd encountered in his brief army career had nothing on her.

Late that evening, just as it grew dark, he came to see me once more. "You think you ready to leave now?"

I asked if he could give me maybe one more day. Incredibly, I was really enjoying the conversations I was having with Rachel. There was so much I could teach her and it was obvious she didn't have much chance for intelligent conversation where she lived. I did want to be just a little steadier and maybe a little fatter before we moved on though.

What about the girl Luke was with? Would he be able to come with me when I left? She didn't come across as the sort willing to let go.

"Not to worry. I told her the army had assigned me to escort you to Memphis. They know I ain't got no choice."

Which also explained why he didn't have to tell the family he'd deserted; they thought he was still on duty.

Two day later, we left my sick quarters leading a mule Luke had somehow acquired that would carry our blankets and provisions. Luke had said his goodbyes the night before and his girl was hanging on to her mother's hand now and looking all brave. Just before we departed, Rachel broke free from the other members of her family, threw her arms around me and gave me a kiss. I didn't know what to think. I couldn't imagine I'd ever be coming back this way again to see her, she not being a Catholic, but, of course, I did.

The Hillbillies

We didn't make much time that first day, both because I needed to rest often and because our road now went constantly up and down over steep hills.

We were in the Cumberland Mountains, Luke explained. For the most part, our path, invisible to me, lay along the ridges with incredible scenic views of the land below. Sometimes we'd walk across a flat rock strewn area and other times we'd be on a narrow ledge poised over a steep drop. Hickory and aspen grew all about us, though never thickly enough to impede our progress.

The closer we got to Luke's home, still in the mountains, the slower we moved. Without warning, he would pause in midstride, listen, then bring his rifle slowly to bear on the nearby vegetation. Only after he recognized that the sound was that of a bird moving about in the underbrush, would we be off again. His behavior was very similar to that he'd exhibited when we were hiding from the troops just after leaving Manassas.

"Not all the folks around here is friends. Some is downright dangerous. Why do you think I joined the War?"

I soon learned this was because his family and the Jenks had been at odds for generations. And when Bill and Mordred Jenks signed up to fight for the Union, that was it for Luke and two of his cousins. Off they went to fight for the Confederacy.

Late one afternoon, Luke announced we'd be stopping early that day, though he'd told me earlier that we were getting close to his home.

I no longer needed to stop to rest, at least, not as often, and with plenty of daylight left, why couldn't we go on? True, the night came quickly in the hills we walked through, one moment it was light and the next dark as the sun dropped into a valley, but not as quickly as all that.

"Got to see a girl," Luke said, which as far as I was concerned more or less explained our stopping. What I couldn't understand was why we just couldn't go knock on the girl's door, why I was expected to stay behind with the mule. Did he think I'd try to steal his woman?

"She's a Jenks," Luke said, which made even less sense, as everything I'd heard about the Jenks so far had branded them as quite bad people. I'd sort of imagined their women would be cut from the same cloth.

Luke was not about to explain the discrepancy, so I remained in the circle of pine trees with the mule tethered close by, reluctantly but faithfully obeying his instructions not to light a fire and to stay hidden at all times.

Easy enough to do while it was daylight, but when night fell with the moon not yet over the horizon, my only company was the mule that I could hear but not see and the "who?" of an owl off on the night's hunt. Each breath of mine was a puff of smoke on the chill night air and I dearly wished I were home eating a warm bowl of pea soup in which from time to time, one could dip a warm slice of *mere*'s fresh-made bread.

I was asleep and awake and asleep again when Luke finally returned, a warm presence in the darkness. I could only guess he was grinning, because I heard him say, "Yup, she remembered me all right," before I fell asleep again.

The next day I met Luke's parents.

They weren't much for talking and they weren't much for hugging, but somehow all sorts of jars of canned fruit and pickles, and that bread I'd dreamt about, appeared on the table without any real fuss being made. Didn't take screaming and hollering, the way my family would have carried on, to let Luke know they were proud of him and glad that he was home.

They may have been glad to see me too, for that night I had a bed to sleep in, though it was outside in a shed. Moreover, my own clothing being little more than shreds by that time, almost-new replacements appeared by my mattress the next morning and if the new clothes weren't exactly my size, they were close enough, Luke, his father, and his brothers all being perhaps a half a head shorter than me.

I hadn't expected such hospitality. Indeed, I'd half expected them to stare at me, as I was so different in so many ways from their son. But those differences appeared to have vanished on the journey. Now, we both looked like vagabonds with untrimmed beards and straggly moustaches. Nor did I bother to wash my hands before coming to table. What would my parents say? I seemed to have forgotten all I'd been taught of manners.

The next few days we spent doing little more than resting up and eating till we were fit to burst. Soon enough though, we were given chores and expected to earn our keep. When we weren't doing chores, Luke set about teaching me to hunt, which meant learning to fire a rifle. I soon could hit an onion set upon a post, though not at a great distance, and I was useless with squirrels. Once, I even missed a fat, slow-moving grouse that emerged suddenly at my feet.

In the evening, Luke would take off for an hour or three just at dusk, though never for less than an hour that I figured was about what it took to get to and from the home of the Jenk's girl. Most times, he returned with a smug self-satisfied smile, though just as often he would come back with scratches on his face and arms.

One night, I was sitting playing cards with Luke's mother and father, when we heard three shots off in the distance. Ten minutes later, Luke returned. His clothes were torn—he'd obviously crawled through the underbrush, and he was favoring one shoulder. His face was a mixture of dirt and blood.

Surprisingly, his parents said nothing to Luke, though his father smiled at me and said, "jus' courting," as if this explained everything.

When one's best friend, and I guess this was what Luke now was, goes off to see his girl and says he needs you to carry a rifle and watch the trail behind him, well I didn't have much choice.

Besides, while I still couldn't hit a squirrel's eye at a hundred yards with a bullet as Luke could, I could probably wing a man a few feet from me or at least slow him down considerably.

73

Once again the next evening, I was left on my own in the woods near the Jenks' place as the night closed over me, though now, with the help of the rising moon, I was able to see the Jenks' house just over the rise, hopefully without being seen in return.

A half hour passed; owls came and went on the hunt, and strange rustlings could be heard as field mice ran through the darkness to escape them.

A figure emerged from the shadows near the house, gradually separating into two figures, one in pursuit of the other. The bigger stronger figure, a male, soon caught up with the slender female in front of him and threw her to the ground.

My orders were to remain hidden, to act only to save Luke, but still I felt it necessary to intervene. I could not permit rape to take place in front of me.

"What the hell you think you're doing?" the girl cried out when I'd wrestled Luke from on top of her. As soon as she was on her feet again, she began to beat on me with her fists and would have done me great harm had not Luke hauled her away.

"You'd best go now," he said.

Stumbling through the trees, only occasionally losing my way, I slunk back to my stall under the stars. The following day, I went down the mountain.

Williamsburg

On my descent from the mountain, I was conscious that many eyes had me under observation, although no one spoke with or intercepted me. Somehow or other, I was still under Luke's protection.

I'd a pair of fresh boots, courtesy of Luke and his family, and I'd not left hungry—Luke's family were conscientious feeders, but I was starved, nonetheless, by the time I arrived some hours later back in the thick moist air of the Cumberland river valley.

The night before, waking in a sweat, I'd realized, perhaps not for the first time, that I'd spent these many months on the road with Luke because, like him, I wanted to escape the terrible memories of war. Now, it was time for me to return to the battlefields, to resume my role as spy and my responsibilities as a war correspondent. Letters from me to my family, to Jacques, to the Captain, and to the editors of my papers were long overdue.

Late that afternoon, I came to the town of Williamsburg, Kentucky only to realize after I'd sought out and found the telegraph office that I was inside Confederate territory. No communications with my home were possible except via England, a sea journey that would consume as many or more months as had already passed while I was on the road.

If I was to report to the Captain, I was faced with the near impossible mission of passing undetected through Confederate lines and then into Union territory. Fortunately, for good or for bad, the war soon came to me.

The streets of Williamsburg were filled with the men of the 20th Tennessee Infantry. Not surprisingly one of them chose to speak to me. Why was I in civilian clothes when there was fighting to be done?

"*Bon Jour*," I began in reply and proceeded to explain in a deliberately heavy accent reminiscent of my father's that I was a journalist from Bas Canada. The soldier and his comrades thought that was right interesting. Did I take photographs?

Apparently, men were to be found everywhere in the war area who specialized in taking pictures of the men in uniform that could be sent home in letters to relatives.

I apologized for not being one of those men. They said this was O.K.; I could come along with them anyway.

Unfortunately, they were heading south rather than north in the direction I was going. Regardless, they wanted me to come along with them and I thought it best to comply. Undoubtedly, they had stories to tell of interest to my readers. Besides, their request was more in the form of a command.

The soldiers' story, typical of a time of war, was that they had been asked to march north for some time and now had been directed to march south. The way they explained things, the whole useless charade was sort of a large-scale marching drill, only instead of parading back and forth on a field with the fifty or so men of one's company, they marched now with ten thousand others. As always, little rhyme or reason could be discerned in the army's movements.

"Colonel Battle, he knows."

"He don't know, only the General knows and he ain't telling."

I was not to meet this Colonel Battle, though he was to learn all about me, but I did meet that same day with Sergeant Ewen of the 20th Tennessee Infantry regiment and then with Lieutenant Peyton, and then, though very briefly, with Captain Gooch.

The Sergeant was the first to ask to see my papers. "You're with the Union," he exclaimed when I handed them to him and I received some very hard looks from the men around me.

I explained at some length how I'd first been credentialed as a correspondent in Washington and that I wasn't on one side or the other but was there in the field to report on the bravery of Sergeant Ewen and the men of the 20th Tennessee Infantry.

Privates Johnson and Crosthwaite were assigned to keep watch on me while the Sergeant said, "he'd look into it."

One couldn't imagine a more physically distinctive pair, yet so alike in mannerism and general attitude. Private Johnson was short, rotund, and had an unfailingly cheery disposition. Somehow, he'd managed to continue to gain weight despite the rigors of army life. A fact explained each time we ate together when he polished off not only the food in his own mess tin but any tidbits, however nasty looking, that his comrades in arms appeared reluctant to eat.

By contrast, Crosthwaite was extremely tall and so thin he looked barely able to manage his rifle. His mouth drooped at the corners; as a result, you might think him depressed, but his droll comments were the source of much of Private Johnson's and my amusement, and all the while the expression on his own face remained unchanged.

For some, army life might be something to be endured, but these two appeared to find joy in its every aspect, including their latest assignment, that of guarding a suspected Union spy. Light-hearted they might be, but every time I considered wandering off to freedom, I saw that one or the other's eyes were set firmly upon me.

I had the opportunity to repeat my story to Lieutenant Peyton that evening and, much later, after I'd spent the night more or less under arrest, with Crosthwaite and Johnson taking turns snoring, I got to hear the Lieutenant repeat the gist of it to Captain Gooch.

By that time, I'd also had the opportunity to walk a good many miles side by side with the men of the 20th, first south into Tennessee and then back again north into Kentucky after marching some miles further to the west.

We settled finally in a campground near the town of Mill Springs, on the south bank of the Cumberland River. After which the Captain, and the Lieutenant, and Privates Johnson and Crosthwaite walked me over to what was clearly their regimental headquarters. Here, I was marched back and forth in front of an open tent flap to be inspected like a prize cow by still more senior officers. The observer that sticks out in mind had a bushy white beard, an equally full mustache, and a broad sunburned forehead. Perhaps, this was the Colonel Battle the men had spoken of.

An hour passed and then the Lieutenant told me I was free to walk about the town and to talk with whomever I wanted as long as I stayed within the limits currently occupied by the brigade.

77

Just like that, I was free, at liberty, alas, to search out my own meals, as the army would no longer be responsible for feeding me. And free to find lodgings where some officer had not already located his bed. My escorts, Privates Johnson and Crosthwaite, likewise were told they were free to resume their normal duties.

While the pair were no longer watching me, it was clear somebody was. On the first day or so of my "freedom,' these watchers were in uniform. Thereafter, they were in civilian clothes, trying desperately to remain invisible, though the constant reappearance of those same faces wherever I walked could hardly be coincidence.

I realized that the Confederate command did think me a spy, but were less interested in me than in my possible contacts, as many Kentuckians were Union sympathizers. The widow who gave me lodging, the tavern keeper who poured me ale and let me eat of his lunch may well have become objects of suspicion.

The day came when a man with a handlebar mustache dressed in the clothes of a drover approached me in a tavern and offered to buy me an ale. As we chatted, he asked if I might not have some news to impart. I though it imprudent to explain that I would not have any news of real interest till I was back behind Union lines and able to relay the Union positions to men like Captain Tom. I longed to shout, "Yes, I am a spy, but for your side." But I knew this would do me no good. So as I remained silent, my eyes vacant, this particular agent provocateur went away unsatisfied.

After weeks of the men of the 20th Tennessee regiment standing about, playing cards or performing unnecessary drills, late one evening, the sound of bugles could be heard throughout the camp. The men were lined up for an hour or so in the cold rain, before they and I set out along Mill Spring Road toward the Union positions.

We marched for six hours in the darkness, along a road that rapidly turned into a sea of mud. Just before daybreak, we heard the sound of musket fire somewhere in the distance ahead of us. Later, I learned that our dawn raid had come as no surprise to the Union forces, and the first probe by our cavalry had met with stiff resistance.

Although there were said to be more of us than there were of them, we were spread out for miles along the narrow muddy road, slowing our advance, and were never able to bring all our forces to bear.

The 15th Mississippi was in the vanguard and I later heard the following, possibly made-up story from one of their number: They'd been approaching the enemy under cover of a deep-wooded ravine where they could be heard but not seen. This so infuriated the Union commander that he climbed up on a fence, brandished his sword, and demanded that they stand up and fight like men. The Mississippians were eager to oblige, but after advancing some further hundred yards, almost flanking the Federals on their right, their advance stalled.

Most of the soldiers had never been in a battle before, and the dark rainy morning, coupled with the smoke and din of battle and the lack of visibility in the dense woods, produced quite a bit of confusion. General Zollicoffer, leading our brigade from the front with the 19th Tennessee Infantry, was sure that his men were firing on another Confederate regiment, and he rode forward in the road to reconnoiter. A half-mile further on, he encountered a Union Colonel who had ridden to his right for the same purpose. Neither recognized the other. General Zollicoffer was said to be extremely nearsighted, and his own uniform was hidden from the Colonel's view by a raincoat. Anyway, Zollicoffer ordered the Colonel to cease firing on his friends. The Union Colonel, assuming Zollicoffer was a Federal officer whom he did not know, and unsure of who the troops to his right were, answered that he would never intentionally fire on a friendly unit. As he moved back toward his own regiment, a member of Zollicoffer's staff suddenly rode out of the woods to warn him, firing his pistol at the Union officer. The Union soldiers immediately returned the fire, and both General Zollicoffer and the man who had come to warn him fell dead in the road.

By this time, our regiment had come up to the front and along with the 15th Mississippi launched a series of furious attacks on the Union's position, some even reaching the fence, where they fought the Federals hand-to-hand. Bayonets were poked through the fence rails, and the Mississippians attacked swinging the long knives they used back home to cut cane.

As the skirmishers began firing, a few minnie balls began to sing about the men of my adopted regiment and some of them began to duck their heads. Colonel Battle cried out, "Don't dodge men; don't dodge!" A shell came screaming through the woods about this time and passed uncomfortably near Colonel Battle; naturally, he dodged. His men began to laugh at him, and he called out: "Boys, only dodge the big ones, not the little ones."

The men of the 20th Tennessee were armed for the most part with obsolete flintlock muskets that carried three buckshot and one round ball. In the heavy rain, almost all their muskets misfired. My former guard, Private Crosthwaite, and several of his companions first took to cursing, and then to smashing their useless flintlocks against the trees.

We should have won. We had a numeric advantage in troops. But as at Bull Run, the shells from unseen artillery began to crash among us without warning. By the time we'd regrouped—these men were incredibly brave, the Federal forces had brought up reinforcements. The battle continued but I was already moving back down the road in the direction I'd come.

Shortly thereafter the entire company was forced to retreat to keep from being surrounded. Lt. Peyton was killed when he refused to retreat or surrender, but stood firing his pistol at the advancing enemy. Private Crosthwaite, Sergeant Ewen, and Captain Gooch were also missing when we finally reassembled on the other side of the river. In all more than a quarter of the regiment were killed or wounded, among them Colonel Battle's son.

Just as well that I was not able to get in contact with Captain Tom in Montreal. The battle was a total rout for the Confederacy. Not only had our troops suffered heavy casualties, we had been forced to leave behind all of our artillery pieces and wagons, and most of our horses and camp equipment.

And, in my own panic, I'd completely forgotten my original objective and was trapped still behind Confederate lines.

Nashville

My return to Union territory came in the most unexpected of ways when I was captured along with the City of Nashville.

The death of so many men of the brave 20th in the Battle of Mill Creek now permitted me a certain measure of liberty. In the confusion created by the mass exodus of men and horses from the scene of the carnage, I was able to move freely and as rapidly as I could away from the encampment where my movements had been restricted for so many weeks.

Only gradually did the realization dawn on me that although I had a great story to report, I'd no way to report it. To turn about was impossible given the press of retreating men behind me. I needed to go forward and quickly too, but in which direction?

For several days, I stayed with the decimated regiment as Colonel Battle led us back across the river and through the mountains. But sooner or later our paths had to diverge.

I came by chance upon a soldier as he stood shivering holding the reins of a horse, looking as if he very much wanted to be somewhere else.

"Lieutenant disappeared," he said by way of explanation.

I offered to take his place for a short time. Relieved, he handed me the reins and quickly disappeared into the bushes.

I'd learned a great deal from Luke in the months we'd been together. In an instant, I was aboard that horse and on my way to a still undetermined destination.

I wasn't sure how long I would have the opportunity to ride rather than walk—too many steeds had been taken from me in the past—so I galloped as quickly I could through the retreating men, ignoring all demands to stop and receiving a fair number of curses from those I splattered with mud in my wake.

Despite the speed of my moving horse, occasionally a hand would reach out in an attempt to unseat me, for the fleeing soldiers were as desperate as I to escape.

At that point I had my second stroke of luck—though, as always, luck is what one makes of it—and I found myself next to a wagon driven by one those photographers the men had told me about.

A group of soldiers were gathered near the wagon examining a photographic plate the man held out to them. Agreement was reached, finally, for the soldiers handed the man money (which he immediately  pocketed) and he wrote their addresses on a piece of paper.

As he passed by me on the way to return his camera to the wagon, he asked if I might like my photo taken also. I told him I would not and he simply continued walking. But when he found me waiting still on his return, he cursed me roundly and asked what the devil I wanted.

"I'm a correspondent for Le Canadien," I told him. "I think I might get more money for my columns if I could supply my editor with photographs."

"And what would I get from this arrangement?"

"Whatever my editors are willing to pay you."

He said nothing then, but climbed back upon the seat of wagon where he remained silent for some twenty minutes or so, as after I'd once again mounted my stolen horse, we traveled side by side. Finally, he seemed to have come to a decision, for we began to talk as we rode along together in as comradely a fashion as if we'd been friends since the beginning of time.

He was on his way to Nashville, he confided. While taking photographs of soldiers was remunerative, he felt that the photos he would take of public buildings and munitions works would be every bit as rewarding with a great deal less risk involved.

How wrong he would prove to be, but again, I am getting ahead of my story.

I said I agreed and would like to learn more about the photography trade. Could I ride along with him and assist him whenever possible? Of course, my real reasons were to use his presence to provide some sort of cover for my own and his wagon as a last resort should my ride be taken away from me. My horse was a good one and would very likely be pressed into military service when we next encountered an organized military company.

He was not quite the fool I took him to be and the deal we ultimately struck involved an exchange of horses—for my stolen mount was much the superior, in return for training in the photographic art (that is, I would become an unpaid assistant).

I had heard something of Nashville from the men of the regiment and was glad it would be our destination. The truth is that I feel more comfortable in cities than in the countryside, and had longed for some time to be in a metropolis that might well rival the cities I'd already visited.

Unfortunately, the poor condition of most bridges as well as the muddy, poorly maintained roads lengthened our journey well beyond my expectations. Each time we reached a town, my companion would bring his wagon to an abrupt stop, bring out his camera and solicit whatever business he could. We would stop too on occasion in what appeared to me to be raw wilderness, so that he might capture the scene on film. "In Europe, they treasure paintings. Here in the South, it is the land we prize."

We reached Nashville finally, after some weeks, and unlike the poor soldiers we'd deserted had eaten well en route mostly as a result of my friend's occupation.

Despite the many lavish descriptions I'd heard of this supposed western capitol of the Confederacy, Nashville proved no competitor to la ville de Montréal. True, like Montreal, it was located on a river and the bridge we crossed to reach it was an impressive one. But if one restricted one's count to white faces and excluded soldiers, then Nashville had perhaps less than a third of the population of my own birthplace.

True, the city was home to several institutions of higher education, two theaters, and five newspapers, and might well deserve the title,

"Athens of the South." (In which case, Montreal surely ought be known as the "Alexandria of the North.")

It also served as home to a meatpacking plant, a cannon foundry, a percussion-cap manufacturer, and the manufacturers of black powder, cartridge boxes, saddles, sabers, and knapsacks.

Not surprisingly, given such resources, it soon became the objective of the entire Union army. I was in a newspaper office, attempting to sell my account of the Battle at Mill Run, when we first heard the news of the fall of Fort Donelson. Within hours, panic-stricken civilians filled the streets and the rich men of the town, including the newspaper editor with whom I had just spoken, jammed the railroad depots in an attempt to leave.

My friend the photographer had already vanished by the time I returned to our lodgings, taking both horses with him. Fortunately, I had no desire to flee. I intended to be here in Nashville and out of sight when the Union troops arrived. Once they were in charge and things had settled down, I could, hopefully, return to my previous careers.

Momentarily, the city's population doubled as the retreating Confederate troops streamed in from the North. Only a short time later they were gone, taking their sick and wounded with them back across the Cumberland River heading for Murfeesborough.

The law went with them. Commissary warehouses were invaded by the lawless and stores broken into. I must confess that I was among the looters desperate to acquire supplies against an uncertain future.

The riot ended with the arrival of Nathan Forrest's Tennessee cavalry. A charge or two with the horsemen's drawn sabers discouraging all but the most foolhardy.

From the viewpoint of my landlady, the army was no less lawless than the deserters and other riff-raff that had owned the streets of Nashville up to this point. Hoping to thwart the arrival of the Union forces coming in from the east, Floyd's troops proceeded to burn the seven hundred foot spans of the bridges I had so recently used to enter the city. And when they left, it was to take with them as much meat and provisions as they could carry.

Fortunately for my landlady and me, a great deal of food and drink was left behind. While I would spend some weeks in limbo, as I was repeatedly arrested and released by the somewhat disorganized Union occupying force, eventually, when telegraph service was restored, I was able to submit my reports to my papers and even to mail several letters home.

The March to Shiloh

During the next few weeks, the population of Nashville virtually doubled due to the arrival of more and more Union troops. Though most were confined to their camps, those one encountered in the streets were drunk and obnoxious for the most part. And we learned to avoid entire parts of the city where the taverns and brothels were located.

Still, the time passed more pleasantly than I might have expected, for my landlady's husband having failed to return on furlough, she became convinced she was a widow and behaved accordingly.

Telegrams came and went from my principals in Montreal. One from the Captain via Jacques contained what at first appeared to be two contradictory instructions: First, reasonably enough given the absence of all communications from me during the past few months, I was to remain in contact with them in so far as possible. Second, I was to remain by my uncle's side and leave Nashville only when he did.

After some moments thought, I gathered that the "uncle" the telegram referred to was General Buell. The two instructions combined meant I was to let the Captain know as quickly as possible when General Buell left Nashville and in which direction he was headed. Ideally, I would also pass on the disposition of Buell's troops when and if the inevitable conflict occurred.

It took a few more weeks before I was able to report to the Captain that I planned to travel to Columbia, KY to meet with some of Uncle's friends from Murfreesboro.

The unexpected response by telegram that same day was that while I was to remain by my uncle's side, if the opportunity arose, I was to travel south to seek out my uncles in Louisiana, Uncle Pierre in Bayou la Fource and Uncle St. Germaine on the street of the same name in New Orleans.

Committing those names and addresses to memory, I tacked on the arm band Buell's adjutant had thoughtfully provided all correspondents and set out for Columbia boarding one of the last of the trains reserved for Buell's troops.

Alas, the train ride lasted only a few miles, the Confederates having ripped up much of the track as they fled, and we were obliged to march the rest of the way alongside the remaining tracks though acres of wheat and cotton.

The sight of two long bridges in flames greeted our arrival in Columbia late the next evening. As a result, we were forced to halt for ten days in a city lacking even a friendly landlady with whom to seek solace, while the least competent engineers I've ever seen made abortive attempts at repair.

Eventually, we, the troops that is, were ordered to wade across the swift-flowing current. We correspondents followed but took advantage of our status to throw our clothes on top of the wagons rather than holding them over our heads. The water was freezing cold, though no worse than the St. Lawrence in July.

One of our fellows, a rotund chap from somewhere near Chicago, whose fat you'd think would have offered him ample protection, turned back—perhaps because he didn't care to be on view bare-skinned, but the rest of us made it, though a few complained that, even dry, clothes made poor towels.

One week and one telegram later, after a fast-paced march, we reached Savannah eighty miles to the south and east on the Tennessee River. Here we waited; this seemed to be the way of the army: March till you drop, then sit and wait. We waited.

When next we marched, it was across land that was little better than a swamp. One looked forward to the rough spots, because while one might stumble momentarily while straddling a plowed furrow, at least one's feet were out of the mud and water.

At Pittsburg Landing, reached four hours later at the end of a long exhausting forced march, the sound of guns told us that an immense battle was in progress on the opposite side of the river. After a lengthy parlay among the generals, General Grant among them, during which, yes, we waited, we crossed the Tennessee. Not by a bridge, no nothing so simple, but via a series of short hops on trestles laid between half a dozen paddle wheelers. Not quite the comfortable float down stream I'd hoped for back in Savannah. In my haste to board the first of the craft—I so looked forward to the ride, not realizing that we were merely to use the boat as if it were a stone one steps on for an instant while crossing a stream, I did not realize that I was the sole correspondent to do so. The more prudent of my brethren remained on shore contentedly out of the reach of Confederate fire.

Shiloh

The night passed without serious alarm. After awhile one grew used to the sound of shells passing overhead at ten-minute intervals. They were fired from the Union ship, the Tyler, and while our men slept through them, I doubt if the rebel troops on the receiving end were able to do the same.

Exhausted as we were, we all got a good night's sleep, if waking at 4 a.m. qualifies as a full night. Apparently, we'd missed an entire day of combat and were expected to make up for it.

Our prospects looked dim. On arriving at the shore the previous evening, we'd found some 8,000 men all clinging to the earth below the embankment and looking thoroughly demoralized. We got the usual speeches from our own commanders, but I'm not sure we gained much reassurance from them. If we hadn't fled then and there en masse, it was simply because we were too tired to do so.

Still, give a trained man enough sleep, a cup of hot tea and some bread, with, miracle of miracles, jam, and he is ready to fight again. Bad luck for our advancing skirmishers who were forced to eat their bread jamless.

Our skirmishers had already made contact and our entire division was advancing, when I became conscious that additional union troops had arrived, by steamboat—the lucky fellows, to support us. They'd floated while we'd walked. Who says life is fair?

In the first hours of the battle the day before, Sherman's headquarters had been overrun and his division retired with many losses including an entire battery of cannon. The Confederate armies had suffered enormous losses during the attack as well, but this hadn't stopped them from pursuing the fleeing Union troops. The latter became increasingly disorganized, falling into ambushes, and taking heavy losses.

By afternoon, Union resistance stiffened as the retreating units gradually came under coordinated control. Still, the Union losses were tremendous. An entire brigade of Wallace's 2nd division was surrounded and its men killed or taken prisoner by the Confederates.

And what was General Grant's reaction to this? To attack, of course, which was just what our brigade, including the regiment I'd attached myself to, proceeded to do.

Both sides had been bombarded by rain the previous night and our tents had all leaked to varying degrees. I was particularly fortunate in that all the leaks in the tent of Kentuckians in which I'd found refuge were located at some distance from my bedroll. Fortunate indeed! The Union troops whose positions had been overrun the day before had been forced to retreat carrying only their rifles. Not only had they gone to bed supperless, but they'd no choice but to sleep in the open, and to bear up under the rain and cold as best they could.

For me the rain had been a soothing presence, its sound a lullaby, annoying only once we began to march through the damp underbrush, and my pants, increasingly wet, wrapped themselves like cold tentacles around my legs.

We advanced quickly, meeting little or no resistance. We hadn't expected to advance this far or this quickly, given the rout of the Union forces the previous day. We marched in a silence interrupted only by the sound of the rain still dripping from the trees and the occasional rifle shot from a skirmisher far in the lead. Either the Confederate troops had fallen back to regroup, or, the day before, the panicked Union troops had continued to run from their Confederate enemy far beyond the need to do so.

Eventually the sound of artillery was added to that of the skirmishers' rifles. A few frightened men from another regiment broke through our lines as they fled from the falling shells. One was tempted to trip the fleeing men to teach them courage, but who was I to judge others.

As we grew closer to the Confederate battery, we received the order to advance double quick across a field still strewn with corpses from the day before. Ahead of us, the rifle fire intensified, and the shells began to land amid our regiment with devastating results.

In what seemed like the very next moment, we had overrun the Confederate battery and the men of the Sixth Kentucky were engaged in hand-to-hand combat with the enemy. A moment later and we had won; the big guns were silenced.

The men proceeded to spike the cannons, so that they would be useless to the enemy, and to unhitch the horses, the few still alive, that were used to haul the heavy weapons from place to place. The job was not complete before a seemingly endless series of Confederate troops broke from the woods ahead of us in an attempt to retake the position.

I ran. I ran in circles as it turned out. I ran and ran until, exhausted, I threw myself down behind a raised mound. From the acrid smell of the mounded earth, evident even amid the omnipresent atmosphere of gunpowder, I gathered I was atop a fox barrow.

I was not alone in its shelter; an elderly black man of the wool-headed sort the men call "uncle," stared back at me, shivering. He had to have been huddling close to the ground for, what, two days now. Part of the acrid smell of urine was undoubtedly due to him.

A Confederate soldier came into view then, approaching from the wrong side of the mound. I willed myself still, but the black man proved incapable of it. Worse, he remained staring fixedly at me drawing the soldier's attention to my own huddled form.

"Who be you?" the soldier demanded.

"I'm a war correspondent." I held my arm up to display the armband.

"What's that say?"

"Correspondent." I repeated, realizing he could not read, "I'm here to repeat on the bravery of your unit." He continued to stand in full view with the bullets flying all around him, more foolhardy than brave. "Hadn't you better crouch down?"

But my warning came too late. A shot blew away a portion of his skull and he tumbled to the ground. The next moment, a second Confederate soldier hove into view. He wore a slightly different colored jacket than the first, though with the same drab and shapeless pants. He looked down at his fallen comrade, said, "sorry," and immediately ran off again without looking in my direction.

I pointed an imaginary rifle at the elderly black man and pulled its trigger. "Go away," I mouthed. He merely looked down at the ground, ostrich style, and continued to look down until much later, when the sounds of battle had faded into the distance, I moved away.

Down the Mississippi

For an hour so after leaving the battlefield, I had simply walked without regard to my direction. I was not alone, a crowd of soldiers, their faces as dazed and empty as mine, moved directionless along side of me. Some cursed at random, few spoke with their neighbors. All, except for a few Louisiana troopers in their Zouave uniforms wore Confederate gray.

Behind me on the Shiloh battlefield, both sides were to leave tens of thousands dead, yet at the end of the two days of battle, neither had gained a square foot of territory.

I thought ahead to the battle of the French of Canada against our English landlords. Would we, too, leave thousands of dead on the battlefield, and, when and if support arrived from England, France, West Canada, or the Confederacy would they find no Bas Canadian alive to aid?

Coming to my senses, I asked for directions to the Mississippi.

"You in Mississippi." one soldier replied. When my destination, the river, not the state, was revealed, I was pointed West at a crossroads and proceeded to march in that direction.

Late that evening, I found myself on the edge of a marsh, reluctant to go further in the gathering darkness. When I woke the next morning, chilled to the bone after a long night's sleep marred by only one bad dream, it was to find myself enveloped in a thick white mist. After an hour or so spent shivering, waving my arms about for warmth, the sun finally burnt away the mist to reveal a stream that drained the marsh, and a flat-bottom boat tethered to a cypress nearby.

Though a family of raccoons gave me indignant looks, I waded out to the boat. After emptying it of rainwater (a difficult task while I was still carrying my boots to keep them free of mud), I got into the boat and began to pole my way forward. My task was made easier as the stream widened till finally I was able to let the current alone take me forward.

Unfortunately, much of the morning was spent backtracking, as the stream, shortly to become a river, led off in many places to cul de sacs created by beavers taking advantage of the recent rains. (So much for my belief that the beaver is strictly a Canadian animal.) The herons, who shared fishing rights with the beavers, stared at me fixedly each time I struggled to turn my boat about, but never offered any assistance.

Eventually, the main branch of the stream widened to the point I could lay down the pole, relax, and just enjoy the woods around me. The sun told me that I was heading in more or less the right direction and I just let the current do the work.

I was hungry and though, in theory, plenty of food was for the taking: turtles sunning themselves on the bank, fish that broke the surface of the muddy water in pursuit of water-wading insects, and even the occasional deer (venison on the hoof) glimpsed through the surrounding trees, I had neither rifle nor net with which to catch them.

I imagine the hawks circling high overhead felt almost as frustrated and hungry as I did, though in their case, from time to time, one would swoop toward the level of the trees and emerge carrying something in its beak.

A town went by on the north bank of the river, and then another one. Each time, I considered stopping, perhaps see if I could buy the makings of a meal, but each time, I could not quite overcome my fear of human complications.

Day gave way to night; I slept fitfully, curled up on the still damp bottom of the boat and then, abruptly, I was hauled along by a still faster current and found myself heading in a new direction on a wide river spotted with lamp-lit barges and one huge brightly-lit double-decker paddlewheel heading directly for me.

My pole was useless and I could only pray that the bow wave of the paddlewheel would shove me toward the riverbank and out of its path. I bumped against a barge, unseen till that moment, was roundly cursed, and then invited to step aboard where I would no longer be a menace to shipping.

For the next hour, I lay, a useless supercargo, against a stack of rails. The bargemen were kind enough to share their breakfast of coffee, bread and cheese with me, and within the hour, the first leg of my trip down the Mississippi River came to an end with our arrival at Memphis.

I saw little value in taking lodgings there, but had no choice for I needed time to file my reports and purchase a complete change of clothing. Fortunately, the second letter of credit the Captain had supplied me with was accepted at the bank, it would have been denied less than a week later when the Union took control. I checked into a hotel, took a bath, and put on my new clothes. After visiting the telegraph office, I made my way still red-eyed back to the pier to see if I might purchase transport to New Orleans on a southbound steamboat.

The clerk informed me that while I might buy a passage south from him, my trip would be subject to interruption, priority being given to the passage of troop ships, and though I had a ticket, I might still have to yield my place on board to an officer or a diplomat of the Confederacy.

The clerk leaned forward and confided, "The troops all move north now and while you will very likely get safely to your destination in New Orleans; your return passage can be not be guaranteed."

He was wrong, of course. I would have to disembark between Vicksburg and Natchez, where Confederate control of the river ended, and make my way further down the river by raft. He was wrong, too, about the soldiers, who had already begun to abandon Memphis steps ahead of a Union bombardment.

Having little alternative, I bought my ticket and after two more wonderfully filling meals at my hotel, presented myself for departure the following day. No ship was in evidence, so I returned the day after, and the day after that until finally a paddle wheeler sat waiting at the pier willing and able to take civilian passengers south.

Once on board, I went below as quickly as I could to the salon, figuring I would be less likely to be bumped in favor of some other, more important (and/or wealthier) passenger if I were not readily available. Indeed, when I went on deck again some hours after our departure, three Confederate officers had come on board and three of my intended fellow passengers had been forced to depart.

The richly furnished riverboat had lost a good deal of its gloss in the first year of war. The mahogany panels in the salon had initials carved in them and bullet holes could be seen here and there in the outer wall, though these had been patched with plaster and covered over with whitewash for the most part.

"The Union skirmishers take potshots at us from the cover of the wooded riverbanks," confided the elegantly dressed elderly man who stood next to me at the railing. I flinched involuntarily, but he said the shooting was more likely to take place further down the river, this stretch being firmly under "our" control.

We exchanged pleasantries and I learned he was travelling on behalf of a meat packing plant in Chicago. "Big meat eaters, these soldiers." He didn't actually sell meat but was on board as a representative of the company. "The government's a slow payer and if we are to maintain our cash flow, we must sell shares in the company, don't you see."

I said that I did not and he took the trouble to explain how companies like his were financed. The stockyard took money from its shareholders; it used these monies to purchase the meat it sold to the government. When the government paid the company, each shareholder would receive back a minimum of ten times their investment.

I was reflecting on the value of putting capital to work in this venture, when a second man, with a gimpy leg, clearly acquired in battle, walked over to us and announced that he would like to purchase one hundred shares.

Other passengers followed his lead and so I was denied the immediate opportunity to arrange a loan with my new friend so that I might purchase one hundred shares for myself. I later learned that much as he might have wanted to accommodate my need, by law, share transactions had to be cash on the barrel. Thus, lacking immediate capital, I lost all chance at might well have been a most profitable investment.

Encountering the man with the gimpy leg later that evening, I learned he had financed the purchase of his own shares through sales of a miracle medical cure. He thought that I, too, might benefit from its purchase. I remarked that I was then in excellent health, and he quickly inquired if on occasion I suffered from headaches, shortness of breath, liver problems, gas, or incipient baldness. When I said "no" to all the above, he asked whether my father might not have lost all his hair at a young age. If anything, my father and grandfather are plagued by the need to get constant haircuts lest they look ill groomed. After I related the bad news, he wandered away to chat with someone else.

My third and last profitless encounter that evening was with an elderly man who had been sitting off in a corner by himself reading from his bible. He was not unusual in this respect. A great many of the passengers on that boat carried bibles to which they referred from time to time. In Canada, the only ones likely to carry and refer to a bible are priests and seminary students.

(Of course, my mother, like all women, carries a rosary, but this is something quite different.)

The days on board passed quickly with similar encounters though eventually I found myself left alone as a result of my lack of capital for shares, need for miracle cures, and interest in bible passages. One man did attempt to sell me a bible, which he said was richly provided with the original illustrations, but, again, lacking funds, I had to say no.

Those men not to be found strolling on deck were likely to be spending their time in the salon playing cards. Caution dictated that I refrain from such an amusement. In the weeks I'd spent in the company of the men of the 20th Tennessee, I'd seen many of the men play cards, and I'd learned many, many ways to cheat at the game, but had never become adept enough to put any of the methods I'd observed into practice. Fortunately, I found more than enough excitement in the happenings along the banks of the river and in the water itself.

The Mississippi was in full flood from the melting snow further north and had overflowed its banks in many places. The recent heavy rains had only contributed to the problem. To the usual river traffic, in itself an object of fascination was added a variety of objects swept along by the raging waters. These included chicken coops, sometimes with one or two squawking fowl still poised on top, loose boats, and planks that might well once have been part of someone's home. Just as it was getting dark on the second evening of the voyage down river, I was sure I saw a corpse floating by. Perhaps not. For some time, my memory had been playing tricks on me; I often heard the sound of cannon and men's screams though absolutely no one was about.

Vicksburg

At Vicksburg, we learned that our boat would not be travelling further as safe passage could not be guaranteed. The disembarking passengers were a surly bunch, barring the fortunate few whose principal destination had been Vicksburg. None were quite as panic-stricken as I, or so I thought at the time. The town was filled with soldiers coming and going, marching in tight formation. The few solitary men in uniform stood on guard, rifles at the ready. Vicksburg at War was not a place for anyone without a solid excuse for his existence.

I might be able to convince them I was a correspondent; I had the necessary papers stamped by a Union Colonel. Then again, I might not and would find myself in jail or, worse, forced to take an oath of allegiance to the Confederacy and wear a uniform myself.

Some of my fellow passengers had remained on the wharf casting about for someone who might be willing to take them further south. But I thought it best to beat a prudence retreat south along the riverfront until, well away from any soldiers, an opportunity to travel further presented itself.

Several carriages passed me—perhaps some of the passengers had been successful in getting transportation—or perhaps, these were just the carriages of townsfolk returning to their plantations. But after a mile or so of walking, I was alone on the road.

A few ramshackle cabins that sat along the riverbank could be glimpsed through the trees from time to time. I wondered how they had fared during the flood. Once or twice, I made my way down to the river only to glimpse a swiftly moving current that spilled over the bank from time to time.

Finally, upon one of these excursions, I came across a boat that had been pulled well up on the bank, safe from the flood. Oars and poles lay close at hand and I reasoned that a good push would soon get me on my way.

Before thought could way to deed, a small boy and an even smaller girl appeared suddenly out of the bushes.

"You want a ride, mister?"

I said that I did.

"Gold piece."

I said this seemed a high price to pay just for a ride. Meanwhile he had dragged and pushed the boat most of the way into the water and one at a time had lifted and fitted the two oars each of which appeared to weigh almost as much as he did.

"Gold piece. Final offer," he said in imitation of some adult he must have overheard.

I reached out a leg as if to step aboard and he pushed off the boat into the current.

"Not so fast. You give the gold to my sister, first."

The whole situation seemed so entirely improbable. I did need a boat, but the child seemed an unlikely oarsman to escort me downstream. Besides, it looked as if despite the boy's best efforts, the boat was on its way downstream already.

The branches parted a second time to emit a tall man with long scraggly hair and a beard that pretty much covered all of his face but for an opening through which his stained and crooked teeth leered offensively. "You trying to steal my boat?"

"Not at all." I replied, making what I hoped was a disarming motion with my hands. Keeping one eye still on the man, I looked over at the river and saw that the point was moot. The current had already carried boy and boat some hundred yards downstream and the boy's frantic efforts at rowing were of no avail.

"He was daddy, he was trying to steal your boat," the girl chimed in.

"Damn you. Gimmie that gold piece." he snarled with not a word about his soon-to-be missing child. The man moved toward me threateningly and I took off running back in the direction of Vicksburg. When I paused finally it was to find my boots mud-splattered and my pant legs covered with burrs. But I'd outrun him.

Slowly, I continued to make my way back to Vicksburg. Hiding by the docks, I waited until dark before I ventured out of the shadows onto the wharf.

A group of my former fellow passengers, the bible salesman among them, were engaged in conversation with two scruffy-looking individuals. The latter were about as attractive as the river rat who had chased me earlier.

Not seeing anyone in a uniform, I moved within hearing range. Apparently, the men had a boat, and the group was negotiating to be taken down river. Some were already reaching for their wallets when a chubby red-faced fellow spoke up: "I ain't gonna pay you till we reach Baton Rouge."

"Sure ye will, after we take ye there, and you escape ashore without paying." said the smaller and scruffier of the two men. "Cash now."

"Let's see the boat." This request came from the bible salesman.

"You don't trust us," said the two men together, trying to sound as if being distrusted wasn't an everyday occurrence for them.

"Let's see the boat." cried the group in a chorus.

Finally, the bible salesman negotiated a compromise: We would pay our fare once we were on board and on our way down river.

Several hours passed while we huddled in the darkness near the wharf. I expected arrest at any moment, for the sound of revelry could be heard in the nearby taverns. A press gang was a press gang whether or not its members were intoxicated.

But those sounds died abruptly when the watch came and cleared the taverns; clear heads had been ordered for the next day's maneuvers.

The two men we waited for appeared suddenly out of the darkness. For an instant, until I recognized the pair by their scruffy appearance, I feared arrest. Again, they demanded money. Again, the passengers, speaking as one, told them, "No."

Fortunately, they really did have a boat, an ugly barge of the sort used for hauling livestock up and down the river. Its odor immediately gave it away. I hadn't expected better, though some of its prospective passengers complained. It was a boat and I knew boats like this could navigate the river.

Before we could step on board, the men again demanded their money and again we refused. Not until we were in mid-river did we get out our wallets and line up to pay. Only one of us had succeeded in paying when a circle of lanterns appeared suddenly in the waters around us and naval gunboats and ship's launches could be seen on either side. "Hove to," a voice cried and a warning shot rang out over our heads.

Instead, the man who'd been collecting the money leaped overboard. Suddenly, our barge was adrift, the towing boat having taken off at high speed.

Fortunately, our captors nudged us up against the shore before we'd drifted too far, after which we were transferred to the navy ship and then to an immense warehouse. As far as odors went, I couldn't detect much difference between the place we now were being held and the barge we'd just left.

They let us sit on the floor for an hour or so, after which we were taken away one by one to be interviewed in an adjoining room. I never saw any of the other men again.

"And what is your purpose in traveling south?" asked the taller of two extremely weary naval lieutenants. Their uniforms may have been starched and cleaned much earlier that day; now the pair just wanted to go home.

"I'm spying for the Confederacy," I reported, equally weary. I just didn't care anymore. I was tired, thirsty, and wanted to go home. My only cheering thought was of a 14-year old girl with her aunt's reading glasses back in the mountains; no, she must be 15 now.

"Another con man," the other lieutenant remarked to his companion, "How do they tell such lies with such straight faces?" Then he turned to me. "We don't want your kind in Vicksburg. Was up to me, we wouldn't have your kind in the entire South. Now get you gone and if any of Lieutenant's Harold's men or mine sees you again, you'll hang. Understand?"

I understood. And once outside, I set off walking in the light of the newly risen sun toward Natchez and Baton Rouge once more.

Natchez

The trip to Natchez consisted of placing one foot after the other while fleas nipped at my ankles, the part not encased in a dead man's boots. The views were uninspiring consisting mainly of shacks on the one side, half in and half out of the river in many cases, and unplowed fields on the other.

Occasionally a family could be glimpsed by the river, sitting or standing outside their poor excuse for a home, motionless for the most part, with only the children curious enough to venture toward the road. Even then, the kids, barefoot for the most part, would only stand staring until I passed.

All were poorly clothed, emaciated. I wondered why they did not make use of the fallow land across the road where, in many cases, the remnants of last year's crop cotton could still be seen untouched. Perhaps, they did not own the land and, at best, were squatting where their tumbledown shacks sat by the river's edge.

The war was far away from here, yet all about me were its effects.

The city of Natchez didn't seem to know war was raging less than fifty miles away. Oh, I'm sure plenty of the townsfolk had relatives who'd enlisted in the war, but still they were able to go about their business without having to hear or see anything in the least military. And what a dull business theirs was, though Sundays are always most dull in whatever town one is in, even Montreal. If it cannot be avoided, Sundays one must go with one's mother to church, after which one visits one's relatives so that one may be told he has grown so big and asked, again, what grade he is in.

Natchez may have had some beautiful homes, but if so, they had to be far outside of town on some plantation. The steep climb from the riverbank just wasn't worth it. The people I saw were friendly enough but only to each other. Of course, having walked all the way from Vicksburg, I was covered with dust, and not exactly the sort one would invite home to a Sunday dinner—assuming, that is, that these were the kind of people who would extend such an invitation.

I removed a tomato or so I saw sunning itself in a garden—Luke had taught me well, and made my way back downhill again, dragging my heels and feeling mighty sorry for myself.

A raft piloted by two white-haired gentlemen hove into view just as I arrived at the wharf. I waved frantically at them, like a naval semaphore communicating an admiral's orders, every so often pointing downstream in the direction I wanted to go.

My display appeared to have attracted them, for the raft now came close enough that I could holler, "Baton Rouge, take me!" while continuing to wave and point.

Miracle of miracles they brought the raft still closer, though I was forced to run along the riverbank to keep up with their progress down the river.

They were almost alongside and I was preparing to make a leap, when the current seemed to pull them away. This happened twice more. Even though they'd been kind enough to slow their craft when I stumbled and fell, I began to sense their stopping and pulling away was no accident.

Finally, though, they did halt the raft long enough that I could leap aboard.

"Sorry about that, strong current today," the taller one said with a smile, or was it really a vicious grin?

I shortly discovered that the pair, Whitey and John, were inveterate pranksters given to telling equally unfunny jokes. Incidentally, I've no idea why one of the white-haired men was called Whitey while the other went by his Christian name. Maybe that was a joke, too. They were of an age, in their early forties with prematurely white hair, and seemed to be equally responsible or irresponsible as the situation demanded.

Their jokes were terrible. "Shall I take the right fork?" John would ask when the river divided.

"Best to wait till we're served with a spoon or knife," Whitey would reply.

"Spoke to some folks back in Natchez," Whitey said, when he saw he again had my attention. "I hear you're some kind of Union spy."

"Confederate," I responded, straight-faced. The two men looked at me and then looked at each other.

"I think he might be the one," Whitey said.

"Definitely." John responded.

"We want you to be our partner." they said together.

But I was now a wiser man than I'd been only a few days before. "Just how much are the shares in your partnership?" I asked.

They laughed. "We're confidence men, of course," said Whitey, "But we're thinking so are you and you'd make a good addition to the team. How about it?"

"You work the riverboats?" I ventured

"Yep. Whist is our real game. Shouldn't have played poker, at least till John got more proficient at dealing off the bottom. Next thing we knew, they're putting us off the boat at Vicksburg."

"They put everyone off the boat at Vicksburg." I replied, "That's as far as the Rebs control the river."

"Well I'll be." "I didn't know that." the two clucked in turn, while keeping perfectly straight faces. They'd had me again. Or maybe they hadn't. Either way, time passed quickly in their company, and when we spotted the first of the Union gunboats anchored off the river in Baton Rouge, I was sorry to say goodbye.

Baton Rouge

I spent my first night in Baton Rouge in a comfortable hotel, gradually adapting to the lack of motion characteristic of life on land. The next day, I rented a chaise and set out for Bayou La Fource. Located several miles below Baton Rouge, it was sufficiently far away from the six regiments of infantry, two artillery batteries, and a troop of cavalry, which with the Union then occupied the city that I felt sure "Uncle" Pierre would feel free to confide in me the true purpose of my presence in the area.

The residents of Bayou La Fource were Acadians, men and women of French descent, who been expelled by the English from their own country a century ago. I assumed that my French was their French and had not expected that the very first person I met, an attractive bare-foot girl only a few years younger than I, would respond to my inquiring the way to the house of "Pierre, mon oncle," that I talked funny. Nor had I imagined that the town was so lacking in events of interest, that as I walked to my uncle's, I would be followed to his porch not only by the bare-foot girl, but by a half dozen other bare-foot street urchins of mixed race, and several grandfathers, also without shoes.

My uncle also responded to my greeting in French with a statement delivered in his own strange accent that I talked funny. Everyone in the group that had gathered about me on the porch laughed at this and left only when Pierre invited me inside and shut the door.

He told me that the Confederates hoped to regain Baton Rouge, only recently taken by the Union, sometime in the next few months. My task was to report on the disposition of the Union troops and to return as soon as possible to the Bayou with an annotated map of their positions. Pierre would pass on the map to his contacts in the Confederacy. To ensure there would be no misunderstandings, we switched frequently back and forth from French to English as we talked.

Taking Baton Rouge was the key to driving the Union out of Louisiana as Confederate soldiers could then launch attacks along the Red River on Union-occupied territory as well as threaten Union control of New Orleans.

5,000 men led by Major General John C. Breckinridge had already entrained from Vicksburg for Camp Moore where they were to be joined by a small infantry division led by David Ruggles. Simultaneously, the Confederate fleet was sailing down the Mississippi River on its way to engage the Union ships near Baton Rouge.

With a wink, Pierre also passed on to me a one-page letter that had been folded and refolded many times as it had been forwarded first to Jacque by my parents, then to the Captain, and then by a yet more circuitous route to Bayou La Fource.

A crushed leaf adhering to the page bore only a trace of the scent of the Cumberlands that it had once held, enough so that I easily determined who was the sender. Her message was in the form of a rebus. I rejoiced at its content.

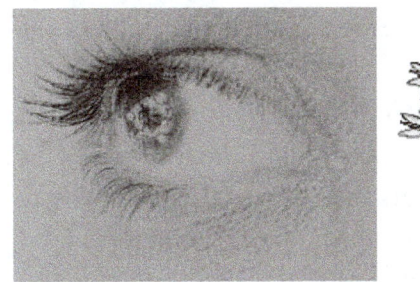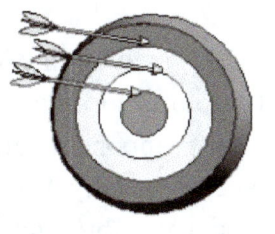 U

Well?" Pierre wanted to know. But my only reply was a smile which I'm sure he understood.

To encourage my early return to the Bayou, I was invited to partake of a savory stew. Foolishly, I inquired as to its composition and learned that it incorporated snake, sausage, and alligator meat. The fried chicken we had as a second course along with a mixture of tomatoes and okra was revealed to be frog legs. I didn't care about the food's origins—it was delicious and I took advantage of the invitation to eat as much as I could.

One thing only disturbed me. I soon realized that not only were the French of Louisiana not prepared to help their cousins in Bas Canada obtain their freedom, they were unaware that we needed, much less that we desired to be free of the English yoke.

Regardless, once back in Baton Rouge, I faithfully carried out the task I was assigned and soon returned to Bayou La Fource bearing not only the desired map but the welcome news that the Union invaders were new to war, having been in training for only two weeks before being sent to occupy the city. Of even greater comfort was the news that the supplies the troops had brought with them would last for several weeks at best.

Not long after, not much longer than the interval necessary for the news I'd brought to be passed on, General Breckinridge moved his men to the Comite River, just ten miles east of Baton Rouge.

Of course, the Union forces under General Williams had their own spies. On the afternoon of the fourth, he received information from some Negroes that the rebels were approaching in force. At half past three on the following morning the reveille was beaten, and, the Union troops were marched out from the center of town to meet the enemy.

The Confederates were lined up in two divisions, north of the city. The action occurred around Florida Street, and began with the Confederates pushing their opponents all the way back across town. Bitter fighting took place, especially around Magnolia Cemetery.

The initial engagement was brought on by one of the companies of the Twenty-first Indiana, which was on picket duty about a mile back of the camp, being driven in by the rebels.

As soon as the firing was heard, General Williams sent the other companies of the Twenty-first Indiana to the support of the pickets. On reaching the scene of action they found that the enemy was in too great force to contend with successfully and had no choice but to fall back to the front of their tents, followed by the enemy. There, they made a stand and engaged the entire brigade of General Clarke, consisting of two Mississippi regiments, and a third regiment, composed partially of men from Mississippi, the rest being from Arkansas. The fighting at that place was very severe. The Indiana boys kept the enemy in check for a considerable time but eventually, they were ordered to fall back, which was done to the distance of several lacrosse fields.

Just about this time the right wing of the Union army consisting of the Sixth Michigan and Nims's battery was engaged by Colonel Allen's brigade. Simultaneous with this movement the Union left was attacked by Ruggle's brigade. The fighting at this point was excessively severe, and the roar of battle was heard all along the line from left to right. This lasted for about twenty minutes, during which time the rebels kept their troops masked under the cover of the woods as much as possible, while the Union soldiers were exposed to their fire in the open field. Considerable further inconvenience was experienced by the troops, in consequence of their facing to the east, which caused the looming sun to shine in their faces.

At one period of the fight the Confederates got into the camp of the Twenty-first Indiana and burned it, upon which this regiment, from the cover of the woods, poured a most terrific volley into them, doing fearful execution, and causing them to retire precipitately. They met a similar fate from the Twentieth Maine, into whose camp they had forced an entrance, though the Confederates succeeded in burning this camp, too.

While the fight was raging, three companies of the Sixth Michigan Volunteers were in peril of being cut off by the Fourth and Thirtieth Louisiana regiments, commanded by Colonel Allen, acting as Brigadier-General. These two regiments suddenly emerged from the woods and marched toward the three companies, with the view of turning their right flank. They succeeded in capturing two guns belonging to Nim's battery, and a well-known officer, named Henderson, was seen to wave a flag in triumph over the guns.

The captured cannon soon were brought to bear on the Michigan regiment. But the latter lay flat on the ground, so that the Confederate balls flew over them. In the subsequent lull, the Union troops poured a well-directed directed volley into their enemy's ranks, handsomely seconded by the remaining guns of Nim's battery. The latter, while making a detour along the road, so severely galled the Louisiana regiments by a well-timed cross-fire that when the two companies of the Michigan Sixth came to the bayonet charge the rebels were driven back to the cover of the woods, leaving the two guns they had captured behind them. Nims' battery thus got their own again.

The hardest part of the fighting was in the center, where the Fourteenth Maine fought with distinguished bravery. The Twenty-first Indiana also fought like tigers, and one of our generals paid them the handsome compliment of saying that but for those damned Indianans Baton Rouge would have been captured, though many of the half-dead and terrified Union soldiers do not see it exactly in that light.

The Union commander, Brigadier General Thomas Williams, was killed in action and his adjunct Colonel Thomas W. Cahill took over. The Colonel led a retreat to prepared defensive lines near the Penitentiary, under the protection of the Union warships. Here, the Confederate troops came under fire from the gunboats, and events immediately began to go the worse for our side.

Standing on the river bank, I saw the Union gun-boats *Essex*, *Sumter*, *Kineo*, and *Katahdin* take up their positions, the two former to protect the Union left and the two latter the Union right flank. The *Essex* and the *Sumter* opened fire in the woods, their shells screaming through the trees, tearing them into shreds and scattering an iron hail around. Signal-officer Davis, of the *Kineo*, stationed himself on the tower of the State House, from which elevation he had an excellent view of the field, and could signal to the vessels where to throw in their shells. After the battle had raged for some time the Union troops began to fall back on the Penitentiary; fortunately, several well-directed shots from the 11-inch guns of the boats kept the rebels from pursuing them. Shortly after this the firing ceased.

At half past three, the firing was re-opened, the gunboats *Kineo* and *Katahdin* shelling the woods in different directions where our troops were, doing great execution. It has been stated that one shell from the *Kineo* killed from forty to sixty Confederates, a figure I cannot quarrel with having witnessed at first hand the effects of artillery fire. Toward evening the firing again ceased, though the gunboats continued to send in a shell every half hour in different parts of the woods during the whole night, with the view of keeping our troops at bay; but they had already fled, the gallant charge of the Sixth Michigan having completed their discomfiture.

The Confederates had been led by Major-General John C. Breckinridge, who scampered off in such haste that he left his sword behind. It was picked up on the field, and was retained as a trophy. Perhaps it was this circumstance that gave rise to the report that he lost his right arm.

While the firing was going on, smoke could be seen up the river behind a bend. I learned later that it came from the Confederate ship *Arkansas*, which had been specifically designed to ram and sink the Union gunboats. This ship was plated with railroad iron on the outside, over a planking of six-inch oak; inside were six inches of condensed cotton over another six inches of oak. Had one of its engines not failed, it would have done considerable damage to any ship it rammed and might well have won the naval battle for the Confederacy.

The next day, I proceeded up river in a small boat manned by two stout and well-paid oarsmen, in time to see the *Arkansas* come under fire from the *Essex*. The rebel gunboats *Webb* and *Music* ought to have come to the Arkansas' defense but fled on seeing the other Union gunboats round the bend.

As the Union gunboats approached several shots were fired at the *Essex* from the *Arkansas*, one or two of them taking effect, but without doing any damage. Lacking an engine, the *Arkansas* could not be turned and was unable to bring more than one of her two guns to bear. The *Essex* ran past the *Arkansas* to a part of the river where there is a reach of some length, and opened on the Confederate ship at five hundred yards with three guns loaded with solid shot. One of these took effect in the starboard bow of the *Arkansas*, which split in two from the force of the concussion. An incendiary shell of the *Essex* commander's own invention was fired, and entered the *Arkansas'* hull just where the solid shot had struck previously. Immediately a jet of flame shot upward from the *Arkansas*, and in a short time the entire vessel was on fire.

Without any prospect of naval support, Breckenridge was unable to attack the Union positions and withdrew. Union troops were to evacuate the city a week later, concerned for the safety of New Orleans, but by then I was already in the latter city.

New Orleans

Before I left for New Orleans, I stopped in once more at Bayou La Force to dine with "Uncle Pierre" and, hopefully to, see the same young lady who had first greeted my arrival. I was disappointed in the latter—apparently news of the letter I'd received had got out, but the food served at my uncle's table was excellent as always.

New Orleans was an exciting city. But for the heat, it reminded me in many ways of Montreal. Like the country of my birth, land that had once belonged to the French, while not taken outright, had been sold from under them. And like Montreal, the old quarter near the wharves that had once held the town's entire population had been expanded again and again to hold immigrants from all nations.

I spent the night in a small pension on Magazine Street close to the docks and, with a small breakfast of rolls and cafe au lait inside me, set out the next morning to see the city. For some time, I wandered through the Quarters by the docks admiring the fancy grillwork on the buildings, the balconies where courtesans once called down to prospective escorts.

Some particularly spicy tomatoes were on sale at an outdoor market near the levee and with the addition of fresh bread supplemented my small breakfast very nicely.

Imagine my surprise when next I ran into the same nice Jewish ladies I'd known in Washington. Over a second cup of coffee, we discussed our respective travels. Melanie, the more attractive of the two sisters sat next to me, and her mother and sister Caroline sat across the round table.

Mrs. Landau was eager to tell her story first and no wonder. The living conditions for her and her family had only deteriorated after the battle of Bull Run while the streets of Washington filled with the drunk and disorderly. All traces of civility vanished from her keepers.

"Can it be wondered that we all felt a despair which language fails to depict? Such a day as followed the Union defeat at Bull Run requires a much stronger tongue than mine. The night the news reached Washington, we few Southerners felt our danger in the return of the vanquished foe.

"We closed our house, put out all the lights, but were too excited to sleep that night. Although we observed this conduct some time after our internment in that dreadful attic, we were charged with illuminating our house at the result of the battle, for which we were arrested a second time, this being one of the charges.

"Finally, our jailers decided that it would be best to see the back of us as we weak Southern women posed so great a threat to them. And, so, abruptly, we were told to pack and go.

"We had hoped to see you again before our departure. Indeed, we had been most disturbed that you had not been heard of or seen since the time of the battle. Had you been killed? Our chaise had been returned to us, of course, but the men who returned it had failed to speak of you. We only knew that you were not among them.

"We left Washington by the two o'clock train, and in a few hours were seated in the steamer bound from Baltimore to Fortress Monroe.

"At the entrance to Chesapeake Bay, we were stopped in order to have our trunks examined. Every piece of newspaper was destroyed that could give 'aid and comfort to the enemy,' but they could not get those that I had enveloped my frozen body in. I had been told that newspapers were great nonconductors of cold, and had prescribed them for myself while disregarding war orders. I think Mr. Davis found these papers warmer than I did, although I cannot tell why.

"At Fort Monroe, the flag-of-truce boat was waiting for us, while a fearful storm raged, and Captain Jones, Federal, said it was impossible for us to proceed. But we were determined to declare our freedom as soon as possible and soon heard the booming of the Confederate cannon, recognizing the little boat filled with friends. News of our departure had heralded us, and a perfect ovation was in store at Craney Island, near Norfolk."

The rest of their journey, while tiring, was without the dread that had overhung them constantly since the attack on Fort Sumpter. They heard me tell my tale of adventure in turn and then, to my delight, they invited me to dinner at their home that evening,

115

Later, when they learned where I was staying, they insisted that I move in with them for the duration of my visit.

"And will my room be under the eaves as yours was in Washington, with the need to stoop low as one crosses the room from side to side?"

They laughed, Washington being well behind them now, but Melanie pressed my hand tightly, an indication that this particular memory was not entirely free of sorrow.

We took their carriage, a new one, first to my pension, and then onto their home in a relatively new area of New Orleans located between St. Charles Avenue and the River. Their house, like the ones on either side of it, was three stories in height, and the flower-filled garden that extended behind it twice the size of the house.

I learned later, that their home, like that of most of the Jews in the city was located within walking distance of their synagogue. I wondered at first if I would be able to eat their food. Fortunately, it proved not all that different from what I was used to, though many of the dishes that I'd shared with my Uncle Pierre such as shrimp jambalaya were not on their menu.

Their Jewish grace at meals was a simple as their grace had been under the eaves in Washington. (It was simpler in some ways than that we observed at home when my mother had been one too many times that week to visit a priest.)

I soon discovered that my chief function in their household, which I cheerfully carried out in lieu of rent, was to escort Melanie and Caroline to a variety of functions, whether to take them shopping for a dress—I would refuse to come into the shop with them but would wait outside—or a fancy-dress ball, though few of the latter were held while I was in New Orleans.

More often, Melanie and I would attend a garden party, sometimes remaining to dance with the others till late, sometimes leaving early together to walk along the levee holding hands.

"My mother would surely disapprove," Fannie once said as we walked in this fashion.

"Mine too." But the walks continued.

Once also, we went on a group picnic held on a large estate further uptown. The grounds were lovely, filled with magnolia in bloom. Yet it was in those gardens, I think, that I was to contact the fever that would keep me in bed for many weeks, leaving me conscious for only part of each day and unable to take care of myself.

When my fever broke finally, and I regained some measure of consciousness, it was find a large nipple poised only inches about my face. A drop of water lay precariously on its tip looking as if it might fall to the bed at any moment. Desperately thirsty, I did the natural thing, brought my head up and took the nipple in my mouth.

"You can let go now," declared a girl's voice, that of Melanie Landau. I opened my eyes fully and releasing the nipple, met her eyes with mine.

"You're awake," she said, and then blushed. "This was the only way we could get you to take liquids. I'll run now and get a glass."

"Must you?"

"Well, it was the other one's turn." Then, it was the other nipple's turn, after which we had relations, and a moment later I was asleep, a real sleep this time.

We had relations several more times after that. Of course, this was only when her mother and sister were not in the house.

In the end, I realized that it would be very difficult to take this girl back to Montreal and explain her to my parents. She was Jewish after all. One afternoon, after we'd had relations again, I explained this to her. I neither expected, nor appreciated her reply.

"Of course, I can't marry you silly. It's only because you're Catholic that we can have relations. If you were Jewish, the right kind of Jew, you know, with money and family connections, it would be out of the question."

Slowly, it dawned on me that her mother and sister must know about the two of us, that they left the house each time we had relations, only so that it would not be known among their friends that they knew.

The Gulf Road

I wanted to go home. I was tired of war, tired of living among strangers. Nothing I had seen or heard in my travels had persuaded me that the South would be successful in its struggle to be free, or, if the Southerners were, that they would rally to our cause.

Finally, I made the long put off visit to my spymaster, St. Germaine. He was a precise little man, finely barbered with every hair in place. His cravat looked as if it had been tied by a manservant as indeed it had. He worked for the state as a criminal judge and must have put fear in the heart of every miscreant that appeared before him.

His scorn-filled gaze soon told me that I, too, had been judged and found wanting. Apparently, my presence in the city had been known for some time. He wondered aloud that I had not reported to him before. "We are at war. You are a soldier even if you do not wear a uniform. You cannot just neglect your duties."

"And are you prepared to help us, afterward?"

"I do not know about that. I do know that while you have been going to balls and garden parties and cavorting in the bedroom with that Jewess, the Union blockade has grown tighter and tighter.

"For some time, we had hoped to retake Ship Island but so far have failed, despite its being held solely by black troops.

"Your task, still, is to follow the route I give you and prepare a map of all possible landing places where our blockade runners may safely bring ashore food and war materials. While you partied, our troops have gone without food, their rifles without bullets. The Federals have gone from capturing one in ten of our ships to capturing one in three.

"Now, here are lists of the places you are to go, the men and the women you are to contact, yes, women, for the southern woman has proved our greatest strength in this time of crisis. You will stay here in my home the night; in the morning, when these lists are memorized, the originals destroyed, you will go."

118

Only at the last moment and only because I'd noticed the sheet of half-crumpled paper sitting on the edge of his desk did he hand me the second letter from the Cumberlands. Again the message was in the form of a rebus from which I'm sure my correspondent derived as much pleasure in putting together as I did in figuring it out.

In the morning, I was handed over like a sack of potatoes to the two men who were to escort me through the Union lines. They spoke the same bastard French as my "Uncle Pierre" and were as skillful as he in navigating a pirogue through the swamps.

Our trip via back roads and bayous took me through a narrow stretch of Mississippi near the Gulf of Mexico and into Alabama. Only the frogs and turtles that hopped or slid from the muddy banks into the water witnessed our passing. My escorts served no cause, Confederate or Union, only the ties of family. They left me several miles outside the town of Gulfport where I headed immediately for the beach, perhaps too eager to do my assignment. Far out to sea near the horizon, a single patrol boat was the only sign of the Union Blockade.

The Gulf waters hissed as they came and went over a bed of pebbles. Perhaps, I lingered on the beach longer than I should have, intrigued and confused by the odor, so similar too, yet so different from any of my memories. I've lived by water all of my life, midway across a broad river whose opposite shore, though distant, is always visible. Here the water stretched away endlessly until it merged with the horizon.

A gull flew perilously close to my head. A second gull joined the first, angrily screeching until it had driven me from its territory. I continued to walk north along the shore, turning only when a jet of land stretching out into the Gulf blocked my way. I followed it to where a metal-clad lighthouse leant precipitously out over the water.

Ascending the shaky staircase as instructed, I met with the lighthouse keeper, a woman, who had as little use for idle conversation as the Judge, a reflection, perhaps, of her solitary occupation. Still, after advising me that the blockade in that area appeared impregnable and would continue to be as long as the Federals held Ship Island, I was invited to dine en famille with her and her daughter at their home that evening.

Supper was not elaborate, but it was tasty, and the chatter of her eleven-year old kept me entertained. The latter asked after my travels and I reported what I thought was fit for her to hear. The pair laughed loudest when I told them about my first experiences on horseback and how, immediately after, I had stumbled when I first attempted to walk again. (I left out the part on how Luke and I happened to acquire a horse.)

"You think folks'll be asking why you're not in uniform. You been asked before?"

I said that I had.

"Let's see what we can ... if only you looked older....Come with me."

The woman led me out on the porch, told me to sit on a wooden rocking chair and to lean back. She disappeared then for a moment, and when she returned appeared to be mixing up some kind of witch's brew with ashes from the fireplace and whitewash its main ingredients. The next thing I knew she was giving me a shampoo.

The feel of her hands massaging my scalp was arousing. I thought of Melanie and turned my head to look up at the woman.

Those same strong hands twisted my head back into place immediately. "Don't you get no ideas. I'd doing this for The Cause."

Moving to stand in front of me, she wiped my face with a wet cloth, and then showed me in a looking glass the changes that had been effected.

What I saw was more in the nature of a ghost than the elderly gentleman she'd been striving to turn me into. Either way, I guessed folks would no longer wonder why I was not in uniform. What service would want me?

"I made him a sign," her daughter said proudly.

The sign read, "Help me rejoin my unit," in a large childish scrawl not all that different from the handwriting of most of the enlisted men I'd marched with.

"I won't have to walk much with a sign like this one." I said, thanking the girl.

"You'll sleep here on the porch," the lighthouse keeper interrupted, speaking in a brisk tone that indicated the fun was over for the evening. "Skeeters won't be all that bad." A half-hour later she returned with a cup of tea and some netting that she threw over my prostrate form.

As predicted, the girl's sign soon won me a ride the next morning, though I was mentally prepared to walk the distance to Mobile. Ride followed ride. My disguise was working. Once I heard a woman say to her husband in a quiet tone she thought I wouldn't hear, "If this is the best we got fightin', then heaven help us."

The most entertaining ride I had, albeit I was as much the entertainment as the entertained, was given me by an elderly Negro whose mottled appearance suggested that patches of black skin had been pulled away from his head and arms.

I wouldn't have thought to ask him for a ride, in part because his wagon was pulled by a horse almost as elderly as he, had he not looked down as his horse and wagon ambled by to ask, "if the young master would like a ride."

A huge black bible sat on the seat between us and after we'd been underway for a few minutes, he asked if I would be kind enough to read some to him.

Lacking further direction (or much knowledge of the bible apart from the story of Moses and some bits of the New Testament), I chose Jonah. I'd heard the man had been swallowed by a whale, which it made it sound as if his story might be interesting.

121

Turned out there was a great deal more to Jonah's story than the part about the whale and even a couple of useful morals. The first of these was that one cannot avoid one's fate, which in my case meant that whether or not I chose to follow the Judge's instructions, from here on out, I would probably end up following the same increasingly dangerous path.

The second moral of the story of Jonah was that one oughtn't to sweat the small stuff but be grateful for what one had. I suppose for the survivors of Shiloh, this meant be glad you are alive and forget the rain and how wet you are, the mosquitoes and the itches you cannot scratch, the thunder of the cannons in your ears long after the firing has stopped, the gun smoke, the corpses you step over, and the memory of the friends who died all around you.

"You were at Shiloh, were you?" the colored man asked.

I nodded; apparently, I'd voiced my thoughts aloud.

"Which side?"

Without pausing to wonder why he'd even asked such a question, I answered truthfully, "Union," adding as quickly as I could that I'd carried only a pencil and a notepad, not a rifle.

"You think black folks is the same as white folks?"

I gave this question the full consideration it deserved. "Probably not." We rode on in silence after that until he dropped me again by the roadside.

Mobile

Absent a balloon like Professor Lowe's, I'd little opportunity on the road from Gulfport to Mobile to uncover possible landing sites for our blockade-runners. I couldn't ask the people I met along the way for information, lest they think I was a spy for the Union. And though the road often brought me in sight of the Gulf, without that balloon, I couldn't tell how deep the waters were or how close in a loaded ship might be able to get to land.

Perhaps most disturbing was the occasional glimpse of a Federal gunship patrolling the offshore waters. As Judge St. Germaine had said, one in three of our blockade-runners were likely to be stopped and its crew imprisoned for the duration of the conflict.

Arriving in Mobile, I went immediately to the offices of the Steamship line and inquired after the name of the contact I'd been given. A large man with an equally ample belly appeared shortly out of back room.

"I'm Jean-Pierre," I told him. "I need transportation north."

"So you say," he began after which we exchanged sign and countersign.

"We've a couple of alternatives. Best I show you back in my office." He winked at the clerk who'd first waited on me as he maneuvered his belly away from the counter and let it lead the two of us to where we could talk in private.

"We've had fair success in this region." He said, pointing to the map on his desk at a stretch of coast marked in green ink. "Not here; river mouth is too well guarded. But here and here." I traced the positions of the landing spots he'd indicated on my own map of the St. Lawrence River.

"Small boats; small loads; but we've never once been stopped."

He gave me more precise figures on the tonnage and I wrote these down on my map also. The numbers were not impressive; still a few small holes in the blockade were better than none.

After I left his office, I didn't see much of the rest of Mobile, though I was curious about this port city so deep in the South, for the steamer Cherokee left that very evening.

The Cherokee, a two-engine sternwheeler, was shorter and had one less deck than the steamer I'd ridden down the Mississippi from Memphis to Vicksburg. A much larger three-decker with its paddles aft the stern was anchored tightly against the pier nearby, where it lay awaiting repair from the damage it had suffered when it ran afoul of a water-logged tree.

"Water's down; we could have problems," said a boatman as he ambled by. But before I could ask him what these problems were likely to be and how we might overcome them, he was called away elsewhere. On a return trip, he mumbled, "they've had a snagboat clear ahead; not to worry." And though I'd still not the slightest notion of what he was talking about, I devoted myself to not worrying thereafter.

From the Cherokee's upper deck, one could see the island fortifications that guarded the entrance to Mobile Bay as well as the multiple cannon of the old Spanish Fort on the opposite shore. Federal troops would not dare to attack Mobile coming up river from the Gulf of Mexico in the way they had attacked and taken New Orleans.

Almost dusk when we boarded, it grew darker still as we entered the river proper and so, to my lasting regret, I saw very little of the land between Mobile and Montgomery. I contented myself with wandering about the ship, only occasionally being yelled at by a crewman if by chance I'd wandered into territory forbidden to passengers. One could not help but admire the Cherokee's ornate scrollwork and want to see more of the vessel; even its chimneystacks were lavishly decorated.

Whenever the opportunity presented itself, I stole a glance into one of the elegant staterooms in which passengers with a good deal more in their purse than I would spend the night. These rooms were larger and their furniture far more elegant than any hostelry in which I'd spent the night so far.

I found my own bed on deck by a pile of rope and woke only when the steamboat's whistle told me we were about to dock in the state capital, Montgomery.

To Columbus, Macon, and Savannah

So far, my contacts in each of the cities I'd been instructed to visit, Judge St. Germaine the exception, had greeted me with a mixture of fear that they might be exposed, and relief that the intelligence network to which they'd devoted themselves was still functioning.

Not so the grizzled major with the withered leg to whom I turned over my maps in Montgomery the next morning. He was the master player who gave us all our tasks, Captain Tom included.

While he wanted to know what I'd seen and heard, he was as interested in how I'd gotten from place to place, why it had taken me as long as it had, and, to the penny, how I'd spent the funds I'd been provided.

None of my answers seemed to quite satisfy him. This may have been his normal manner or it may have been that despite his best efforts, he still had too much to do, too few people to do it with.

I didn't get in to see him immediately. I was left in the garden of his stately mansion for an hour or so while half a dozen others—were they spies also?—came and went to his offices.

My wait was interrupted twice. First, by a black servant who brought me a highly welcome cup of something very close to coffee. And, an hour later, when the same servant brought me two letters from home.

The contents of the letter from Jacques were unsettling. First, Le Canadien had ceased publication; I should forget about submitting articles to them. The Herald continued to publish my reports—as their readers only wanted to hear about blood and injuries, but surely I could see that my reports of defeats and pyrrhic victories on the Confederate's part did not contribute to The Cause. He concluded with the most unsettling news of all: The Captain had been reassigned and expected to join an active regiment in his own state.

So was I to go forward or stay behind? Already noted was the impossibility of shipping out at the Port of New Orleans, nor was I sure how, even had I wanted to, I could have succeeded in returning there.

I would go forward then as Jonah had, visiting each contact en route as per my original instructions, and hope that by the time I reached Charleston a new assignment (and some money) would await me.

The letter from my parents—clearly one my mother had dictated to my father, said that they missed me, and hoped I'd recovered from my fever. Was I remembering to stay warm at night? (Yes, mother, except when I am obliged to sleep outdoors in the rain.) In a postscript, she asked who Rachel was. Rachael? I touched the two notes I had in my pocket, examined now half a hundred times. I knew only one Rachael, a 14-, no a 15-year old girl in the Cumberland Mountains. Had I given her my address? I suppose I had. And she had written to me! (But no further note with its puzzling rebus was enclosed with my parents' letter.)

The Major could see me now. Question followed question. After he knew everything I knew and some further details I'd been unaware of, he asked how much money I had left.

I showed him. "Not enough," he said. "We need you to go to Fredericksburg."

I told him that my original assignment took me first to Savannah on the Atlantic coast and then to Charleston. This reminder led to my being told to sit in absolute silence for half an hour in a corner of his office while he poured over maps and documents and spoke to several subordinates who came and went from the room.

Yes, I was to go to Savannah and Charleston. As the Judge had directed me, my chief concern was to locate potential landing spots for our blockade-runners. The Major hoped I would be more successful at this than I had been in the past, though he failed to offer any suggestions as to how this might be accomplished.

I was given a very small amount of additional money and told that I would receive more along with further instructions from my contact in Charleston. Then, and it took me some time to realize this, I was dismissed, as the Major continued to work through the pile of

127

documents on his desk, and talk with the men who came and went from the room.

The Montgomery and West Point was the first in a seemingly unending series of railways in various states of repair that I would need board on my return home. Each kept its own schedule; indeed, each kept its own time clock, so that connections among them were often hit and miss.

The John P. King, the engine of the train I boarded, was of standard size, but the passenger car was much narrower than the one I'd ridden south from Montreal. With two seats on one side of the aisle, and only one on the other, it could not have held the regiments of men I'd traveled with on the way to Baltimore.

We left Montgomery early that morning and after only a few hours were required to leave the train in Columbus, Georgia as the tracks of the Muskogee Railroad, which we boarded on the other side of this small town, were of a different width. To conform to the Muskogee's station clock, my fellow through passengers and I were required to set our watches ahead 20 minutes, after which we boarded the new train and settled ourselves into the more comfortable seats of our new and larger passenger car.

About sixteen miles from the town, we passed the scene of an accident that had occurred some days before. At the bottom of a culvert were the engine, baggage car and tender of a train that had been smashed to atoms when the track it was on was washed away by heavy rains. Told that a man and a Negro boy were instantly killed in the crash, we feared for our own safety, but, thankfully, our ride passed without incident.

We passed through the misnamed Fort Valley (no military encampment was in sight and never had been) and arrived that evening in Macon, Georgia where an overnight stay was required. Once again, I had to hunt about in a strange city for accommodation within my means. I can report that the principal and perhaps only advantage of travelling as part of an army rather than on one's own is that one is not forced to search for accommodations in each new location, but can count on the armed forces to provide them.

(When I showed this last paragraph to a soldier on the next day's train, he laughed and said that more than once when supplies went astray, the accommodation the army provided was a blanket on the ground in an open field, "and no roof to keep the rain out.")

I did better than that on my night in Macon, but not much better. Our hostess confessed more than once that she had taken up cooking and boarding lodgers only as a temporary expedient while her husband was away at the War. The tentative nature of her commitment was evident in every inedible bite of the meal she served and in the unswept filth on the floors of her overcrowded rooms, where a large number of uncomfortable ill-made cots had been pushed up against the original furniture.

Confederate troops were everywhere on the next leg of my journey as the Central Railway took us from Macon to Savannah. Many of the soldiers were forced to make themselves as comfortable as they could in open freight cars. Fortunately, the rain had stopped by then. The railroad was still repairing the track in some places and several times the train came to a complete halt. Once, we were forced to get out, walk around the blockage and board a second train that was waiting for us. Still, we arrived in Savannah only a few hours later than scheduled.

Savannah

Savannah is enormous. The walk from the train station to the wharves alone is some 6 or 7 blocks. The first section of the river I came to was lined by cotton gins, few of which were in operation. The Confederacy still had cotton aplenty, but the Federal blockade prevented it from being shipped abroad.

Open tree-filled squares were set at regular intervals among the blocks of houses, where a very few large and elegant mansions looked down on them. The houses on the streets along which the carriages travel are far smaller and set much closer together.

Thus, poor and rich are neighbors, but no resident of Savannah is likely to mistake the house of one for the house of the other.

My friend the photographer would have proved of great value as a companion on this journey. I would have had a photograph of each city I'd passed through—Montgomery, Macon, Savannah, as well as of each locomotive I'd boarded. The photographs of New Orleans, of the Quarters first occupied by the French would have been of particular interest to my family and friends.

Was my friend alive today? Was he still working in Nashville, taking pictures of the factories that had once churned out cannon, percussion caps, cartridge boxes, saddles, sabers, and knapsacks for the Confederacy and now labored equally hard on behalf of the Union? I would not see or hear of him again.

I saw few whites on the streets of Savannah, but their black servants were everywhere. None spoke to me. This may have been due to my clothes and general appearance or simply because the blacks here, as elsewhere throughout the South, speak to Whites only when spoken to.

The black women looked at me disdainfully—why was I not in uniform? The black men would not meet my eyes.

My contact in Savannah resided in one of those large mansions I've described. Its interior was far more elegant than even the building's exterior suggested, though I never got beyond the large ornate foyer whose ceiling rose far above my head. Inviting wing chairs and other furnishings, some treasured from the previous century, and some that might just have arrived that day from England or France, could be glimpsed through an open archway. Portraits of at least three generations of family hung on the one wall that was visible to me. I took a step toward this other room, my eye on a portrait much smaller than the rest, but was intercepted by a black servant. He informed me in the tones one ought use only in addressing a still more inferior servant that the master was in his office and it was to his office I must go.

I heard the door shut and locked behind me, and retraced my steps toward the docks, again admiring the buildings and thinking of the photographs I would have taken had I the equipment with me. The building I sought sat across the road from the muddy Savannah River. Inside, my contact sat with a troubled air amid the silent machines of the cotton gin that once had brought him wealth. He was slumped over an accounts book, his posture revealing how very depressed he was.

"I wasn't like some fools, thinking this war would be over in three weeks, but still, I didn't think we'd be so alone. Where is England with their promises of help? I'll bet there are British manufacturers every bit as depressed as I am, wondering how they can keep their mills going without our cotton. I've complained to our government; I'm sure they've complained to theirs. Their politicians must be every bit as useless as our Jeff Davis."

"You've a strong army," I offered.

"And no navy to speak of. This dammed blockade." He shook his fist out toward the harbor.

The news was good and bad. The Union blockade of Savannah was complete; no ship had got through it in months. Yet Savannah's fortifications were such that an attack from the sea was out of the question, and the upper river remained under Confederate control.

131

Landings were possible along the Florida coast, he told me, but transport by land from those sites to Savannah was almost impossible, the roads, the few that existed, being in very poor condition.

A poorly dressed middle-aged white man looked in at us from the street. My contact shook his head, and the man walked away without either one speaking.

"No work; no work for anyone. Perhaps I ought to enlist," my contact said. We exchanged glances. "Too old."

I would like to have lingered with him by the river with the war far, far away and unlikely to ever arrive. But my masters had prescribed that I go on to Charleston. My return passage home to Canada would lie along whatever path they chose.

Charleston

At both ends of the Charleston & Savannah rail line, I was witness to shouting matches between high-ranking Confederate officers and railroad officials. The source of these disagreements, unthinkable in the North where the Federal Government under Lincoln had long since commandeered railroad equipment for use wherever and whenever the military felt it was needed, was the Railroads' reluctance to forgo profit in favor of patriotism.

Even though a short march by Union troops landing on the coast could easily sever the connection between the cities of Charleston and Savannah—a route vital to the transport of Confederate troops, the Railroads' officers were unwilling to consider alternative routings, or to the stationing of Confederate sentries on board its trains.

Their objection to an alternative route was based on the question of who would pay for the quarter-mile of track required: the State of Georgia? The State of South Carolina? The Confederacy? Or one or all of the three railroads involved? Jefferson Davis was no Lincoln and despite constant pleadings by Lee and other generals had decided to make no decision rather than to risk his popularity.

As for allowing military riders on the Charleston & Savannah railroad, the compromise that was reached after I passed through the system was to allow armed Confederate sentries the use of a handcar in which they might chase after the trains.

One could only pity the sentries forced to do so, for the land though which the rail line passed was a hot, damp mosquito-infested swamp.

A few too many hours later, the C&S Railroad deposited me and a regiment of Georgia volunteers across the river from Charleston proper. The troops and I had no choice but to wait on the ferry, then march through this beautiful city to the terminal of the Northeastern Railway.

I elected to spend the night in Charleston; no, let us be honest, I chose to spend the night. Once again, I was considering stopping here and avoiding the war and the many battles that awaited me should I proceed north to Fredericksburg as my Savannah contact had directed.

I stopped first at the Mill House Inn, but only to ask directions; this hotel, which had played host to Robert E. Lee, was not in keeping with my budget. The accommodation I eventually found was reasonably neat and the food several steps above that shoveled at me in Macon.

Delicious one-bowl meals were served both morning and evening: Dinner was a she-crab gumbo and breakfast a porridge to which one added cut fruit.

Then it was off to the train station where I encountered many of the troops I'd ridden with the previous day, all highly disgruntled because they'd been forced to wait overnight, unfed for the most part, while only a few of their number went forward—the few the railroad claimed they had room for once paying passengers and freight were aboard.

My notepad and blood-spotted armband served to identify me as a correspondent and the officers were as free as the men in sharing their criticisms of the Northeastern and other rail lines over which they were forced to travel.

Unfortunately, when the men did board, only a few of them were able to join me in second class. The majority found themselves riding on flat cars, mere platforms with no material overhead to protect them from the sun. Unsuitable for the transport of cotton, rice, or other freight that might be damaged by rain, yet the Northeastern railroad though these cars suitable for transporting men.

We were spared rain that day thankfully, but for a light sprinkle that was over almost as soon as it had begun, and our train suffered no delay except that caused by a defective locomotive, a delay that only made a long and tedious journey longer and still more wearying. How I wished I had a traveling companion; the hours I spent in imaginary conversations with Jacques and Rachael were poor substitutes.

Whenever I had the chance, I would borrow or purchase a newspaper, though I was seldom pleased by what I found in its pages. Most of what I read was pure speculation, reflecting the editor's hopes with utter disregard for the facts. Seldom have any battles been as one-sided as those these editors portrayed; brave men had died, but seldom had men died bravely. The results of grapeshot and rifle fire are invariably ugly.

We changed locomotives in Florence when we boarded the Wilmington & Manchester and gained a little in speed. But as we headed through North Carolina, the engines of the Wilmington & Weldon's Perseverance appeared to be too weak sometimes to move our train at all.

I found this difficult to understand.

The Wilmington & Weldon was one of the most important railroads in the South, being the main line for carrying supplies from the Deep South to Richmond and the main route for sending supplies offloaded from the blockade runners from Wilmington to Richmond. Regardless of its importance, or the impatience of its passengers, or the need for Lee to gather additional troops and supplies in preparation for the forthcoming struggle for control of Fredericksburg, those worthless engines required us to spend 20 tedious hours aboard the train before we reached the Confederate capital in Richmond Virginia.

Here we added a few cars carrying iron for the construction of a gunboat and continued on the line of yet another railroad whose name now escapes me. Later that day, we switched rail lines yet again, without the need to change cars, though the sergeant of a party of soldiers that boarded at this point looked as if he might like to throw me and all civilians clear of the car. Finally, close to dusk of the second day, we arrived in Fredericksburg.

A railway official attempting to exert his authority here would have been shot immediately by an exasperated military. Unknown to the passengers on our train, the territory between Fredericksburg and Richmond we had just passed through was already at war.

Yankee cavalry had first destroyed a portion of the track of the Virginia Central road. Then, a detachment of this same regiment had moved on towards the Richmond, Fredericksburg & Potomac Railroad, near Ashland, where they'd remained in ambuscade, to wait for the trains they knew must soon arrive. In the afternoon, an ambulance train came on to Ashland from the direction of Fredericksburg. Its engineer was more than a little startled by a sudden salute of firearms, as a number of bullets passed in unpleasant proximity to his locomotive. Possum like, he fell as if wounded, but to no avail; the Yankees approached and finding the engineer unhurt compelled him to proceed to Ashland with the train. Fortunately, he was able to effect his escape soon after arriving there and came on to Richmond the same night.

Besides the sick and wounded on the ambulance train were a number of citizens of Richmond including a few ladies. They were treated with comparative kindness by the marauders who did not disturb the ladies or the invalid soldiers, and left the ambulance train unharmed. They did destroy a wood train, the locomotives "Thomas Sharp" and "Nicholas Mills," as well as a very small amount of track.

From Ashland, the Union cavalry went on to destroy more railroad property, first on the Richmond, Fredericksburg & Potomac Railroad, and then, a second time, on the tracks of the Virginia Central. They also destroyed a considerable quantity of Government stores, a train of freight cars, and some buildings.

The day before when we'd passed through the area, the cavalry had made contact at the Meadow Bridges on the Chickahominy with the locomotive *Augusta* of the Virginia Central, which was on a reconnoitering expedition. The Yankees had the locomotive nearly surrounded before they were discovered, but the conductor and engineer succeeded in effecting their escape through the swamp. Two Negroes remained with the locomotive, but afterwards escaped and got back to Richmond as well. The Yankees set fire to the bridge, a not inconsiderable structure, and as it burnt the *Augusta* was precipitated into the water.

They attempted to strike the Richmond & York River railroad late yesterday afternoon, but were met and driven back by a portion of Wise's brigade.

Why they'd missed striking at our train or the track on which it ran will remain a mystery, though one no greater than how I already had survived so many battles.

Chancellorsville

My first task now that I was at the scene of the forthcoming battle at Chancellorsville was to locate Lee's headquarters and offer my services in spying on the Union positions.

This proved difficult to accomplish, both because Lee was on the move, and because all sorts of gentlemen seemed employed by Lee only to thwart my objective. "Who was I?" "Who had sent for me?" (Not, "Who had sent me?") "Did I have an appointment?" My answer to all these questions was the letter of introduction supplied me by Major Carp during my brief stay in Montgomery, which described me, my past efforts, and the new purposes I might serve.

Each individual in the command chain need study this document closely, and then compare my appearance with that of the individual described in the document, before passing me on to his superior in turn.

Although, I never actually got to meet with Lee, I did get to hear from him. An adjacent in a Lt. Colonel's uniform rode up while I was waiting for yet another hearing with yet another indifferent senior officer and told me to follow him; we were going to see General Jackson.

The adjacent looked about as if expecting that I might have a horse hidden about my person somewhere, and when he saw I did not, pointed to his own steed. I hesitated before joining him; his right sleeve was tied back at the elbow and it seemed a miracle that with only one arm he should maintain himself in the saddle much less be responsible for both of us. An angry red streak across his cheek marked where a pioneer's musket ball had creased it on the way to smashing his upper arm. Luck was not with this man.

But I had come too far to back down. An instant later, I consigned myself once again to the back of a horse, clinging to its rider, destined to jounce up and down uncomfortably for an hour while we rode rapidly through woods and across fields in pursuit of a General who at that instant already was leading his troops forward into battle.

Hare and deer scattered before us, a glimpse of tail vanishing behind the trees all that could be seen of the latter. Once, we startled a wild turkey, the largest bird I have ever seen, which suddenly rose into the air beside me nearly dislodging me from my precarious seat behind the Colonel.

The battle was already in progress by the time we drew near Chancellorsville and I was to view only the tail end of the resulting devastation. Somehow the enormous army assembled by Union General Hooker had remained ignorant of Jackson's impending attack until he had driven through them. Tents were still standing, camp-kettles were on the fire full of meat destined for the evening meal, and everywhere were the corpses of men who'd reacted far too late to defend themselves.

We caught up with our own men finally making our way through them until we were abreast of General Jackson and his adjutants. Here the Colonel let me dismount so that I might gather my footing before approaching the General. Looking back, I realized it had been wild ride indeed, for the Colonel had lost his cap revealing a rapidly receding hairline.

Jackson had halted his forces here amid the trees on the edge of an open field so that they might regroup before launching a renewed attack. I watched as a line of our Confederate troops marched out into the field, the front-most men holding a Union flag aloft. Such a deception would never have been practiced at the beginning of the war and I took the use of a false flag to be a sign of the increasing desperation on the part of the Confederate generals.

This orderly advance was greeted initially by cheers from the Union forces already in position on the field. I imagine they assumed, in error, that here were reinforcements. This illusion was soon shattered as thousands of Confederate muskets poured fire into their lines.

Alas, the answering Union volley came not from muskets, but from a dozen or more canon perched on top of the hill ahead.

139

Hundreds of our men lay dead in an instant. A second discharge left hundreds more dead and dying.

Many retreated and I admit to moving further back into the woods. But the majority of the well-disciplined Confederate troops flattened themselves against the ground, preparing to advance a few yards at a time between volleys until they had reached the canons.

This was not to be. The cannon balls were replaced by canisters of grape shot and few of the men in the field were left unwounded.

As it was already dark, Jackson ordered a retreat, satisfied with his gains and no debt preparing for a further advance the next day.

I remained where I was, content, if necessary, to make a passive entry behind the Union lines when their troops advanced toward us into the woods. For a moment, I'd forgotten that I'd yet to speak with the General, yet to arrange for a channel by which I might communicate any knowledge I might gain of Union positions. Perhaps, I'd not forgotten. Perhaps, I'd quite another object in mind from the very moment I'd boarded the first train north. By merely continuing to walk northward now the battle was over, I could go home to Bas-Canada, to my family.

Realistically, this would be the best and safest thing for me to do. A thought struck me: Whether I stayed or left, I'd best destroy the letter of introduction I'd been given in Montgomery. If it were found in my possession when I fell into Union hands, I would be shot immediately as a spy.

If so, my death would have been in vain, the result of an adolescent whim to be seen performing something significant. Win or lose, I knew now what a war in Bas-Canada would mean to my people. We would win battle after battle just as the Confederates had —for, like the Confederate Rebels, we French of Canada were determined to win. But each time we fought, whether a battle ended in victory or defeat, many of us would die. As battle followed battle, our numbers would decline; the desire of those surviving would fade. In the face of the continuing advance of our oppressors, every gain ultimately would be nullified, and every life lost from the beginning to the end of the war would prove to have been lost in vain.

Escape was best. I hurdled the dead—let their comrades bury them—and headed deeper into the trees.

Though the sound of gunshots had long since died away, it was soon replaced by a crackling sound as the acrid smell of wood smoke filled the air. The underbrush, dry as tinder, had been set afire by spent cartridges and now the trees themselves were ablaze.

I was not alone in the woods. Grey and blue uniforms could be glimpsed fleeing in every direction from the advancing flames. But which way to run?

Suddenly a man screamed, his clothes on fire. The pines that grew all about us were full of pitch and rosin and, with the air about them now hot as a furnace, had simply burst into flame. Foolishly, I ran toward and not away from the burning man.

A Union soldier was already at work trying to rescue the young soldier writhing on the ground. For an instant, his rolling body would suppress the flames beneath him. Then he would turn and the flames would spring to life again. He screamed the entire time until he lay still and unmoving.

The flames were everywhere. Johnnies and Rebs beat at each other's clothes united against a single enemy. Sparks singed hair and arms wherever the skin was exposed. Finally, five of us fell back out on the path again, including the Union soldier I'd first seen, his hands

141

blistered and burned from his efforts in trying to help others. Three rebels in singed uniforms stood near me looking as frightened as I felt.

I soon saw why. A company of Union soldiers had come up on the double quick to see if they could offer assistance. Their rifles were pointed directly at us. A moment later and we were marched away.

The Lieutenant in charge was all for shooting us immediately, but the Union soldier whose hands had been burned came to our aid.

"They helping. They tried to save Bert." (Bert, I suppose was the young soldier with the penetrating blue eyes I'd seen writhing on the ground. My own scorched pant legs were the result of trying to save him and the other wounded men.) "Give them a chance."

The chance they were given by the Captain who next arrived on the scene was to swear an immediate oath of loyalty to the federal government and exchange their gray uniforms for blue ones. Two of the rebels accepted immediately. The third man said he was a stretcher-bearer and a surgeon's aid; he'd gladly do the same for the Union, but he wouldn't carry a gun.

The Captain said the Union had a job for a surgeon's aid too, and the man would be going off to work in a hospital that very day. He winked at the Lieutenant as he said this and I wondered what could be that bad about this hospital.

"Just who are you?"

This last question was directed at me, and I guess at that moment everyone around me began to wonder, rebel as well as Johnnie, just who the man in civilian clothes was.

"I'm a correspondent, from Canada," I explained, trying on my French accent again despite my lack of recent practice.

"From Canada, eh?" The Captain said. "You got you a pass?"

I said I did not and he said that was O.K., they were just a green back each and he would write me one. I reached for my outer wallet and handed him a bill. The signature of Jefferson Davis looked up at both of us.

"You got any more of these, Reb?"

A few moments and the balance of my Confederate currency later and off to the hospital I went in company with the surgeon's aid.

Arrest and Release

The "hospital" at Point Lookout may have been a hospital once, but was now being set up as an immense camp for Confederate prisoners. They say that by the end of the war, 50,000 men were interned in the prison's narrow confines. When the surgeon's aid and I arrived, we numbered only a few hundred in all, and though we lived outdoors in tents, our cots were widely separated, and the food we ate as good as that the men received in the field.

We just weren't free.

My new job was a simple if dangerous one, since the patients I worked around in this hospital, the part that was still a hospital, suffered from various fevers. From time to time, one of us would catch one of their diseases and become patients ourselves. I didn't come down with anything myself in the next month, perhaps because I'd already suffered with these same fevers elsewhere.

I really couldn't complain. Far from the battlefront, this place was free of the sights, and sounds, and smells that characterized the field hospitals. Though death and dying took place all around us, we needn't endure the constant screams of the injured and the men undergoing surgery. We orderlies emptied bedpans; we didn't trundle wheelbarrows full of amputated limbs.

All in all, my life was relatively comfortable in the short time I spent there. Any suffering I experienced was on the lengthy trip south to the Point and on my need to live and relive the what-if's each day.

What if I had retreated with the rest of Jackson's division? I might have gone with them to Gettysburg, witnessed the greatest Civil War battle of them all.

What if I had ignored the screams of the soldiers trapped in the burning wood? I might not have been on that path when the Union reinforcements arrived; I might have got clean away.

A sojourn on the Atlantic Coast south of Washington in June is a fairly pleasant one. Those prisoners that came later, the surgeon's aid among them, were forced to spend the winter on the Point with only a tent for shelter and inadequate food. More often than not, they died a slow death as they came down with chills and a fever from which they would never recover. I, because of my early arrival and early departure from this prison to be, was truly fortunate.

Men who'd as soon see us dead amid their fallen comrades as walking ahead of them at bayonet point had escorted us from the battlefield at Chancellorsville. I'll admit I brought many of the subsequent problems on myself by trying to explain to anyone who would listen that I was not a Confederate soldier but a Canadian correspondent. This obvious "lie," as our Union guards saw it, only made me the more despicable, the more likely to be on the receiving end of a poke with a rifle. I soon learned to keep my mouth shut, so that when we changed guards, twice, in Washington, the new arrivals more or less left me alone. At least, I wasn't harassed any more than any of the other prisoners that gradually joined us on the long march south to the end of the peninsula.

We started out in wagons, tossed aboard like sacks of grain. But our guards soon figured out it would be more fun to have us walk behind the wagons through the horse shit, while they sat up in the wagon bed and pointed at us with their guns. "Bang, bang," one of them would say from time to time and laugh like crazy.

It rained off and on, but we just kept marching. The way I saw it, this wasn't all that much different than the long march down to Shiloh from Columbus, except, of course, this time, none of us would be coming back.

I escaped from the prison finally, simply by submitting my regular column to the Herald in a slightly irregular way. Specifically, I asked one of the doctors if he would mail it for me and left the envelope open. The man immediately handed over my column and the envelope

145

that contained it to the hospital administrator. Actually, I was lucky the physician had handed it over in so prompt a fashion. I could tell when I entered the administrator's office under escort that he was packing up to leave and might not have had time for me a day or so later.

For some weeks now, fewer and fewer real patients had been arriving, and the hospital grounds were beginning to look more and more like a prison camp. Had I remained at the Point another week, I would probably have found myself digging out latrines for the prisoners, rather than changing bedpans for the patients.

The administrator wanted to know what I was sending in the envelope. (The language he employed in asking was somewhat stronger than recorded here.) "This looks like a newspaper column." Was I a spy? *Mais non*, I was a columnist for the Montreal Herald. He then asked in execrable French if I could speak *la belle langue Français*. We exchanged a few phrases in that language until he ran out of vocabulary, after which he told me in English I was free to go. Best to do so that very day, he admonished, as there were about to be some major changes as the military took over.

I asked if I might ride north with him when he left. He said no; unfortunately, there would be barely room for his family and all their possessions in the carriage that would take them to his new position.

Still, he was able to provide me with some civilian clothes to wear in place of my prison garb (taken from a deceased patient I would imagine). After which, I began to march as I'd done so many times before.

Had I been able to skip from shore to steamboat as we had when crossing the Tennessee at Shiloh, I'd have done so in a heartbeat. Everything I'd heard about the elegant steam packet Georgia that once had passed by the Point every few days on its way to and from Baltimore and Norfolk, suggested grandeur at the limits of my imagination.

Its dining saloon was said to have imported Belgian carpets, velvet chairs with marble-topped tables, and white paneling with gilded molding!

Actually, even if I had proved able to take a train all the way from Washington to Montreal, it was unlikely that I'd have spent much time in dining salons or restaurants of any sort. And my nighttime accommodations along the way would not have been much better than a bench in the park. Before I left the hospital, the doctors took up a collection for me—the doctor who had turned my letter in to the hospital authorities felt particularly guilty, but this money was exhausted by the end of my third day of freedom.

When I reached Washington from Point Lookout two and a half days later, I had just enough cash to purchase a train ticket as far as Baltimore. But how was I to go further? The Confederate currency I'd been supplied with in Montgomery would have been useless here, even if I'd been allowed to hang on to it. I needed to find a way to earn money.

Once again, I started to make the rounds of newspaper offices. The editor of the Baltimore Patriot alone was willing to give me a hearing, though he did more talking than listening. "Chancellorsville is old news. Don't care if you were there when old Stonewall got shot."

He also said "no," practically sneering, to eyewitness reports of naval battles, Shiloh, and Mill Springs. "Tell me about your next battle." he asked, "Where you heading?"

I told him New York first and then Montreal, at which he practically leaped out of his chair, shouting, "That's different, I'll pay for that." An old man who'd been sitting in a corner proofreading turned around and looked at us balefully. I gathered that offers of payment were few and far between at that newspaper. "I'll even pay your fare to New York, if you go tomorrow."

I told him I'd been hoping to take the steam packet Georgia and began to babble about Belgian carpets.

"Ship's too slow; besides, I want you on the train, interviewing the fellows."

He knew something I didn't know, then, and he was happy to share his knowledge with me. "Crazy Lincoln. Not enough he loves niggers, now he wants every workingman to die for them, rich folk excepted. Conscription begins in New York tomorrow. I want you ... I want the Patriot there as eyewitness to when the workingman finally rebels."

The Riot

The next day, I boarded the New York train, fare paid courtesy of the Baltimore Patriot, its editor having been true to his word. His copywriter had been accurate as well, as all else from this editor consisted of vague promises of future payment—if events materialized as promised, if my efforts were publishable, if space permitted.

He'd been right about my fellow passengers heading for New York. They were like a crowd on a trolley car heading for a lacrosse game, ready and determined to root for the away team.

(I'm talking about proper lacrosse of course, not the namby-pamby game I occasionally spied outside the train windows. Proper lacrosse is played on ice, and if the ball and sticks don't draw blood, then the slash of a skate or a fall on the ice or an ice-filled snow bank will.)

Like any team's supporters, these rowdies had their cheers, which they practiced pitilessly, drunkenly, boringly, endlessly without regard to the feelings or the eardrums of their fellow passengers.

"Down with Abolitionists! Down with Niggers! Hurrah for Jeff Davis."

Like Lee marching his troops to Gettysburg, they had come to bring the war to the North.

The immediate object of their wrath, (though, clearly, the Union itself was their ultimate target), was the commencement of the Draft the next day. Or, as the crowd of plug uglies on the train chanted repeatedly, "Rich man's war; poor man's fight."

The draft law passed by the Federal Congress in Washington that spring included a provision that allowed men drafted to avoid service either by paying $300 or supplying a substitute.

I imagine that had such a law applied in Bas-Canada, my parents might well have bought me out so that I could continue in college. This still did not mean that such a law was fair.

New York was the first major city in which the draft was held. The first drawing of names had occurred there the previous Saturday without incident. Sunday, handbills protesting the draft were distributed throughout the city, and early Monday morning the night train from Baltimore arrived with its carload of protesters and me.

Their cheering continued as we paraded along Third Avenue, growing in intensity as we neared the building where the Draft was to be held.

We were not alone. It was a furious crowd of more than 500 people led by the Black Joke Engine Company that began throwing large paving stones through windows and bursting through doors.

A thin line of policeman attempted but failed to drive us back. The rioters rushed in, the clerks were driven out, and the papers were torn up. A can of spirits of turpentine was poured over the floor, and very soon that building and the adjoining ones were in flames. The arriving firemen were not allowed to extinguish the blazes; indeed, the majority of the firemen were on the side of the crowd.

Someone recognized John Kennedy, the police superintendent, standing by in plain clothes, and the crowd attacked him. He was left nearly unconscious, having his face bruised and cut, an injured eye, swelled lips, his hand cut with a knife, and a mass of bruises and blood all over his body. The police drew their clubs and revolvers and charged the crowd in response, but to no avail. We were too many; they were too few.

Arson and plunder became the business of the mostly inebriated rioters. The cry against the draft was accompanied by the now familiar shouts of, "Down with Abolitionists! Down with Niggers. Hurrah for Jeff Davis!"

Hundreds of citizens, found at random in the streets or drawn out of large manufacturing establishments were compelled to fall in with us on peril of personal harm.

I passed a manufacturer's building where an older man with a frock coat and wing collar stood looking out an open window frowning at the crowd below. "Damn fools," he cried as much to himself as to me. "Cut off their noses to spite their face. If it weren't for this war, half of the lot would be out of work. And they want to stop it!"

He paused as if seeking inspiration. "I'm going to wire the Governor." Then he slammed the window down and moved out of sight.

Egged on by the rowdies from the train, the crowd attacked and set fire to a series of buildings including the Hotel York, which, sensibly, had refused to serve alcohol to them, the mayor's residence, and the Eighth and Fifth District police stations. The New York Tribune, a leading Republican newspaper and, thus, a supporter of the draft, was also attacked. Some fire engine companies responded, but most refused to intervene, too many of their members having been drafted on Saturday.

To be honest, apart from the beating of Kennedy, I thought it all to be great fun at first, having little sympathy for either buildings or great corporations. But then the attacks became personal.

The colored population of the city, which were viewed as competitors for the too few jobs then available, were special objects of the crowd's wrath. They were hunted down and beaten mercilessly. Neither age nor sex was spared. Men, women, and children, shared a common fate determined solely by their color.

One man was attacked by a crowd of 400 with clubs and paving stones, then hung from a tree and set alight.

About two hundred Negro children without parents had found a home at the Asylum for Colored Orphans located a few blocks from the draft building at the corner of Fifth Avenue and Forty-Sixth Street. The Asylum was broken open, plundered and then laid in ashes. The children were forced into the streets, some beaten and maimed. The survivors fled in terror to whatever shelter they could find.

A nine-year-old girl from the orphanage, found hiding under a bed, was clubbed to death. I attempted to intervene, abandoning the journalist's role for an instant, and received only a black eye for my pains (though I dealt out many a blow in repayment).

Thankfully, a heavy rain fell that night, helping to abate the fires and send the rioters home. The telegraph wires leading out of the city had been destroyed earlier that day, so my reports on the riot proved to be among the first to be filed. Never mind that the editor of the Patriot changed my lead totally distorting my meaning so that it read, "On Monday, a great uprising of the people led to the Governor of the Great State of New York halting the illegal and unwanted draft imposed upon the peoples of these free united States."

Going Home

What hope was left after seeing what I had seen? What could one wish, what could one pray for? Only that the fighting between the Yankees and their rebels would go forever and that they would never have the inclination to visit their destruction upon the women and children of Bas Canada.

Our English landlords might be obnoxious at times, pompous and indifferent to our needs, but at least they had about them a veneer of culture, of Shakespeare. Their worst elements had been shipped off to the States, whose teeming masses were filled with hate, Iagos, Richard IIIs, and Macbeths.

The final part of my journey, the trip to Montreal, was a mirror image of the one I had taken south three years before. Conductors came and went as the rail line changed. I had time to flesh out my dispatches before we reached Albany, and though not obliged to change trains, I stopped long enough to mail my full report on the riot south to the Patriot and telegraph a summary of events ahead to the Herald. Otherwise, I dozed or looked at the scenery. Only at the border did I get my first reminder of what might lie ahead.

Of course, this many years and adventures after my departure from my native land, I lacked all evidence of my place of origin, but for my accent and appearance. When the uniformed English-speaking functionary asked for, no, demanded my papers, I had none to offer him.

I explained this lack to him, adding something of my adventures, and spoke of my desire to return home, all in French, of course. In a loud voice aimed at the other passengers, as much or more than it was at me or the simple-minded colleague that followed him about, he demanded to know why I could not speak English. "These French of ours," he proclaimed, "Are simple minded."

An interpreter offered himself, and I explained through him that I was Jean-Pierre of the family Mercier.

"They are a large family," the interpreter interjected after making the translation, "with branches all over the province."

"Catholics," the functionary said, "They breed like flies."

"My father is the merchant Julian Mercier."

"His father owns a grocery on Saint Denis." said my interpreter. "He's a fair man, I hear."

The functionary brought his stamp out from within his uniform, but as I offered no papers on which he might affix it, he brought it down angrily upon my extended palm and went on to the next passenger.

I remain convinced that we must never go to war—even to regain our freedom. But if, from time to time, one or the other of the more obnoxious of the English should lose his life, that would be acceptable.

Home and Epilog

A number of letters from Kentucky were waiting for me at home. They contained a large number of misspellings, though the clarity of the writing improved with time, and had clearly gone through many hands and post offices before they reached me from their starting point in the Kentucky hills.

I immediately wrote a single long letter back to Rachael, although all sorts of people, relatives, as well as the editor of the Herald, were waiting to talk with me.

Le Canadien had ceased publication and I'd no hope of collecting my pay. Fortunately, my mother, a shrewd businesswoman, had collected and cashed the checks for all but two of the articles of mine they'd published.

She had even cut out and retained copies of some of my columns. Had I really written after the battle of Bull Run, "One must walk away slowly from the battlefield in order not to draw attention to oneself." No, one must run away as quickly as one can to escape injury or death. Years later, when I was to rise in the middle of the night to get water for a feverish child, I would have the column she'd cut out to remind me that I'd once written, "one cannot realize how important water can be for the wounded; they will cry for it unceasingly on the battlefield, though their canteens may lie just a few yards out of reach. We do not dare to help them; we lie in hiding, cowards, afraid to draw the attention of snipers."

The Herald published and paid for both the summary I had telegraphed and my later more comprehensive report of the draft riots in New York. They went on to employ me full time as a reporter until they ceased publication a few years ago.

Rachael and I exchanged letters for some time. Of these, the most moving was the one she sent that described the siege of Knoxville in graphic detail. The foolish child had traveled to the city on her 16th birthday imagining she would follow in my footsteps as a war correspondent. I could only be grateful that like me she had come away from the dreadful experience alive, still convinced she would make her career as a writer (she had confided this ambition to me during my short stay in the tiny shed with her family) but, like Luke, with no further desire to be anywhere near a battlefield.

This ought to have been the end of the War as far as Rachael and my family were concerned. Alas, Jacque showed up at my door one day in September, shortly after I'd restarted college, full of enthusiasm for another doomed project.

A Lieutenant Young was in town recruiting soldiers for a Confederate raid on one of the Yankee border towns.

"The Confederacy is doomed," I told Jacque. "And they have little or no interest in our concerns. This man was at McGill also to recruit; he doesn't care if the men he leads to their deaths will be English or French."

"Yes, but we are to rob a bank, don't you see. My share will go to our cause. Not to theirs."

I had long since stopped listening and after a while, seeing that I would not budge, off Jacque went on his own. Not hearing from him for several weeks, I assumed he'd dropped interest in the project—Jacque's enthusiasms were always of short duration. Still, I was aware that several of the Lieutenant's other converts intended to go through with it. Everyone at McGill knew. I would have been surprised if the manager of the bank they planned to rob in St. Alban's had not also been alerted.

The raid was a failure, of course, all the robbers but one were captured and sent to jail, and the stolen money returned to the bank. The exception, a young wild-eyed French Canadian, was shot during the robbery by a guard.

The War Between the States ended officially on April 9th, 1885, though scattered remnants of Confederate troops continued to fight on for some months. President Lincoln was assassinated only a few days later. But on April 10th, I was already aboard a train headed for the Union, Kentucky, and Rachel.

We were married twice, once at a small Protestant church near her home, little more than a shack in the woods, that I hadn't realized existed. Virtually every member of her extended clan was in attendance, which included Luke's family as well as the hated Jenks. Our second, or real marriage as my mother would say, was performed by the same priest who had protested so strenuously against my trip South.

We have two children, both baptized, while the oldest is already learning her catechism.

Although Rachel cannot officially attend classes at McGill, I have often snuck her into lectures disguised as a man, and we read and reread Shakespeare together.

My only memories of the War come in our brief spring and fall, when suddenly an odor carried on the breeze will remind me of the fields I once walked through in Virginia, the leaves and ferns that lay crushed beneath my feet as I ran or rode through the forest. The smell of gunpowder is part of the English celebration of *La Règne Victoria* each May and I have as little use for it as I have for *La Reine*.

To purchase more fine e-books like the one you've just read, including *My War*, a pilot's tale of World War II, go to http://zanybooks.com.